P. M. Hubbard and T

››› This title is part of The Murder Room, our series dedicated to making available out-of-print or hard-to-find titles by classic crime writers.

Crime fiction has always held up a mirror to society. The Victorians were fascinated by sensational murder and the emerging science of detection; now we are obsessed with the forensic detail of violent death. And no other genre has so captivated and enthralled readers.

Vast troves of classic crime writing have for a long time been unavailable to all but the most dedicated frequenters of second-hand bookshops. The advent of digital publishing means that we are now able to bring you the backlists of a huge range of titles by classic and contemporary crime writers, some of which have been out of print for decades.

From the genteel amateur private eyes of the Golden Age and the femmes fatales of pulp fiction, to the morally ambiguous hard-boiled detectives of mid twentieth-century America and their descendants who walk our twenty-first century streets, The Murder Room has it all. ›››

The Murder Room
Where Criminal Minds Meet

themurderroom.com

P. M. Hubbard (1910–1980)

Praised by critics for his clean prose style, characterization, and the strong sense of place in his novels, Philip Maitland Hubbard was born in Reading, in Berkshire and brought up in Guernsey, in the Channel Islands. He was educated at Oxford, where he won the Newdigate Prize for English verse in 1933. From 1934 until its disbandment in 1947 he served with the Indian Civil Service. On his return to England he worked for the British Council, eventually retiring to work as a freelance writer. He contributed to a number of publications, including *Punch*, and wrote 16 novels for adults as well as two children's books. He lived in Dorset and Scotland, and many of his novels draw on his interest in and knowledge of rural pursuits and folk religion.

By P. M. Hubbard

Flush as May (1963)
Picture of Millie (1964)
A Hive of Glass (1965)
The Tower (1967)
The Custom of the Country (1968)
Cold Waters (1969)
High Tide (1970)
The Dancing Man (1971)
The Whisper in the Glen (1972)
A Rooted Sorrow (1973)
A Thirsty Evil (1974)
The Graveyard (1975)
The Causeway (1976)
The Quiet River (1978)
Kill Claudio (1979)

The Dancing Man

P. M. Hubbard

An Orion book

This edition published by
The Orion Publishing Group Ltd
Orion House
5 Upper St Martin's Lane
London WC2H 9EA

An Hachette UK company
A CIP catalogue record for this book is available from the British Library

ISBN 978 1 4719 0065 5

www.orionbooks.co.uk

Printed and bound by CPI Group (UK) Ltd, Croydon, CR0 4YY

With gratitude to Faith Vatcher, F.S.A., curator of the Avebury museum. If there are still things I have got wrong, it will be only because I did not ask her about them.

CHAPTER 1

Dick disappeared some time in May, but I did not hear about it until several months later. This was because I was abroad. Also, there was no special reason why I should be got hold of. He was my younger brother, but he had long since come of age, and we were not one of those very closely knit families. I liked Dick, and I had a slightly disapproving and I suppose slightly envious admiration for him. He was an archaeologist and a mountain climber and a great one for the girls. I once asked him which was the most difficult ascent he had ever made, and he said oh, Betty, far and away. After her he reckoned it was a particular crag in North Wales, I forget which. It turned out later that he had at some point made a will leaving everything to what Rupert Brooke called the one before the last. As she had by then settled down as a respectable married woman, it must have been a bit of an embarrassment to her, but I expect the lawyers managed it all very discreetly. Not that he had much to leave, anyway. But it meant that I was not involved in the possibility of his death, even as an heir presumptive.

I say the possibility of his death; perhaps I should say the probability, but that was all there was in it. He had gone out climbing alone and never come back. They looked for him, of course, but he was too experienced simply to get lost or do anything silly. If he had not come back, he had been in real trouble, and the body might have been anywhere in a piece of country like that. I had a letter from the man he was staying with at the time, but, as I say, I did not get it till some months later. It was a man called Merrion. I think I had heard Dick mention him. He was an archaeologist, too, of sorts. I gathered his interests were two or three thousand years later than Dick's, but I suppose they had met on some academic occasion. It occurred to me to wonder why Dick had been staying with him, and I supposed it was the climbing. There were, as I found out later, other reasons. I might have guessed some of them, what with restless, randy Dick and his difficult ascents. The others I could not be expected to guess, not till much later. Merrion had suggested that I come up. By the time I got the letter, the formalities were over, though of course Dick's death could still not be legally presumed. All the same, I said could I come? I still had a month's leave in hand, and some of Dick's stuff was still there. Merrion wrote and said certainly. I went up early in September.

I am not indulging in hindsight when I say it was one of the most extraordinary places I have ever seen. It was called Llanglas. On the ordnance survey sheet it was marked in Gothic lettering *Abbey (Site of)*, which meant that there was nothing to see above ground, only foundations and rubble, and they were buried in the trees. There was a round shallow basin, a mile or more across, with the mountains going up sharply on the west of it and fairly craggy foothills disposed round the other sides. Only one road led to it, winding in from the east between the foot of the hills. The basin was completely full of trees, mostly oaks. The house was at the end of the road, on the eastern edge of the basin. It was built of the local stone, but not particularly old, a hundred years or so. They had not even tried to use material from the remains of the abbey. They had just taken what they wanted from the nearest hillside, which was probably cheaper in the long run. It was not as ugly as it might have been, but it was no beauty.

When I came round the last bend of the road, there was a cloudy sunset going on somewhere behind the mountains. The house and the trees were all in shadow, but there was a sort of top lighting from the colored cloud effects overhead. It made it all look very small, though it was not a small house when you got up to it. It was not really remote, either. There was a biggish village where you turned off the main road, and a market town only a few miles along it. I suppose the last bit of the side road must have been private, but there was nothing to show this. The house was very much on its own, but it was barely a mile and a half from the nearest petrol pump. It was the sort of place a Victorian with money might have built to retire to, especially if he had antiquarian leanings, as many of them had. I drove in between stone gateposts and thought how dark it all looked, with that huge splendor hanging over it. It was an impression I never entirely lost, though there was plenty of sunlight later.

I stopped the car on the gravel in front of the house. It was gray gravel, the same stone as the house was made of, broken up smaller. The whole effect was monotone. A moment later the door opened and Merrion himself came down the steps. I had never seen him, of course, but I never for a moment doubted who it was. He was a very tall dark man with rather staring eyes. Even the skin of his face was dark, with an almost Mediterranean pigment under it. The eyes were the palest thing about him, staring out at me under his dark brows. He carried his face turned down, so that even with his height and with me still in the car he seemed to be looking up at me. I got out of the car. He said, "Mr. Hawkins?" and we shook hands solemnly. I felt he was trying to do justice to what he felt to be a solemn occasion, though I did not feel that way about Dick, who I thought had had a good life and probably ended it very much as he would have chosen.

I said, "Yes. Mr. Merrion?"

He nodded. "Let me help you with your bags," he said. He still did not smile. I found out later that he very seldom did, but at the time I just felt that he was overplaying the thing.

I said, "I'm sorry Dick has given you so much trouble."

I think I wanted to shock him, and I seemed to have succeeded. He checked and stared at me harder than ever. "Trouble?" he said. "Your brother gave me no trouble. I am only sorry it happened as it did." He had a pleasant voice. It sounded like the voice of a much younger man. But he spoke in spurts, hesitating and watching you, and then darting off into a fresh sentence, as if his instinct was to reconnoiter the ground at every step before committing himself. I wondered what there could be in this quiet place to induce such a feeling of stress. I did not dislike him, but I found him, already, a little oppressive. Even before I got inside the door, I was wondering whether I had been wise to come and how long I need stay.

I lost the feeling when I got inside, because the house, once you were in it, was an extraordinarily pleasant one. It was, I suppose, an academic's house. It was not particularly elegant, or even particularly tidy, but everything was easy and comfortable and ordered by a high intelligence. It struck me as a man's house, but this was probably masculine prejudice. I did not know, in fact, whether Merrion was married. Even if he was, I was certain there were no children. There might be a grown-up family, though I doubted if he was old enough to have one. But there was no place here for immaturity.

As we came in, a door on the other side of the hall

opened, and a tall dark woman came to meet us. Merrion said, "Cynthia, this is Mr. Hawkins. My sister."

I bowed and said, "How do you do?" They were as unmistakable a brother and sister as I have ever seen. She was younger than he was, and paler, but the features were almost identical. She had what I suppose some men might call a rather masculine face. It made no concessions, but in her the gray eyes were almost startlingly beautiful. I thought how wrong Cynthia was; it should have been Athene.

She said, "How nice of you to come." The voices were as near as possible identical, even to the pitch, but she had none of her brother's hesitation. Even from halfway across the hall, she was the better man of the two.

I looked at her left hand, as you always do, but there was no ring. She was Miss Merrion, and uncommitted, but I knew one thing from the start. She was not Dick's type, nor Dick hers. If there had been any attraction here other than the mountains, it had not been Cynthia Merrion. I said, "I don't know why I came, to tell the truth. There's nothing I can do now. I'm sorry I was so long getting your letter."

Merrion said, "There are your brother's things. They're still in the same room. You might perhaps—" He broke off, staring at me still with that watchful, slightly puzzled look. He did not know what I could be expected to do with Dick's things, any more than I did.

"I'll have a look at them," I said. "There's probably stuff we can throw away, and I can get the rest packed up, at least. You don't want them lying around. Perhaps I could take them back with me."

Miss Merrion said, "You could, of course. He only brought a couple of suitcases. But there's no need, if you'd rather not. Have a look at them, anyway. Your room's next door. Shall I show you?"

"Please," I said. I picked up my cases and followed her. Merrion stood there, watching us. The stairs ran up from one corner of the hall. To follow a woman upstairs is one of the very revealing things. If they are there to be seen, you see the untidiness at the back of the neck, the awkwardness of movement, the unwanted contours, even a shortage of breath. If they are not, the effect can be very impressive. The effect with Cynthia Merrion was very impressive indeed. She was a rather splendid woman, but not in the usual sense immediately attractive. You wondered about her, but you assumed nothing.

We went along a corridor with doors on both sides. She pointed to one as we passed it. "His things are in there," she said. "You're in here." She opened the next door and went in ahead of me. The room faced south. It was full of the fiery light from the sky, but below the sky there was nothing but dark hills. She went across to the window and stood for a moment, looking out. Then she turned and came back toward me. I still had the suitcases in my hands. She said, "You're not an archaeologist?"

She smiled a little as she said it, as if she did not expect me to take archaeology wholly seriously. "No," I said, "no, I'm an engineer. Much more prosaic, I'm afraid."

She shook her head. "Not necessarily," she said. "You're older than your brother?"

"Only about three years."

She looked at me, not hesitatingly, as Merrion had done, but making up her mind. "You're very different," she said.

I put down the suitcases one on each side of me. The cases and I pretty well blocked the way out between us. She had to stay where she was, and I wanted to have this out with her. "Different how?" I said.

She shook her head again, refusing to be drawn. Then she said, "There's more of you. I'll show you where you can have a wash. Then come down and have a drink."

I stood aside for her and we went out into the corridor again. "Bathroom and loo there," she said.

"I'd really like a walk before it gets dark. Would that be all right? I've been too long in the car."

"Would you? All right. But come in and have a drink when you're ready." She went off along the corridor, but turned at the top of the stairs. "Don't you get lost," she said.

I said, "I won't," and went back into my room.

There was no one about when I went downstairs. There were no lights on yet. The house was still full of the yellow light from the sky, but it would not last much longer. I went straight out of the front door. My car was still standing where I had left it on the gravel. No one had suggested my moving it, and it would come to no harm where it was. I turned and went round the north side of the house. I had not realized how close the hills came on both sides of it. It stood blocking the gap in the hills, straddling the line of the road that came in from the east. Behind it, the great natural saucer swept round in a curve to which the back of the house was almost tangential. The whole saucer was full of trees. I thought the ground dipped from the back of the house toward the center of the saucer, but the tops of the trees lay level between the hillsides, and you could not really tell.

There was no garden. There was a paved court at the back of the house, with outbuildings round it, all gray stone like the house. Beyond them the trees began at once. I skirted the side of the buildings and found, as I had expected, a green rutted track that continued the line of the road and led in through the trees toward the center of the saucer.

I say I had expected it, but it is difficult to say why. I think it was because the thing was so symmetrical and the house so obviously an intrusion. The abbey would have been laid out in the middle of the saucer, with the road leading straight into it through the eastward gap. They liked building abbeys in these hollows in the hills. They had probably cleared the trees from the middle of the saucer, or perhaps the trees had fringed the edge of it then and had moved down only after the abbey was dead. I did not know when it had died. If it was long enough ago, even the oaks could have grown since. I went in along the track and found myself, quite suddenly, in the dark.

I had forgotten how late it was and how much the remaining light came from the sky. At least I could not lose my way. There was only one way to go, straight on into the tunnel under the trees. My eyes could see more now, but there was not much to see. On both sides the space between the trunks was blocked with undergrowth. By daylight there might be ways through it, but in this murk it looked solid. There was not a sound anywhere. Even my feet made none. The ruts were full of moss, and I went, instinctively, as softly as I could. Whatever it was the trees hid, I did not want to disturb it. I thought that where the abbey ruins were there must be at least a little open sky and enough light to show me I had got there. Then I would turn back and go and have that drink. I wanted to turn back now. I did not like the place. I went on precisely because I did not like it. I ply a practical trade and do not easily admit imponderables.

The track led, as I had expected, very gently downhill. I do not know how far I had walked when the ground rose a little under me and then dipped again. Further on the same thing happened again, but this time it was less marked. It was difficult to tell how far I could see ahead. I only know that when I saw the thing standing in the track in front of me, it was already too close for comfort. It was tall and dark and absolutely motionless.

I stopped dead. I do not think I actually stepped

back. I must have made some sort of a noise, because a figure detached itself from the standing thing and came out sideways, looking at me. It was smallish and somehow luminous in the surrounding dark. When I got my wits back a bit, I could see it was human and almost certainly a woman. She had some sort of white coat on. I took a long breath and said, "My goodness, you gave me a fright."

She made a small yelping sound, hesitated, peering through the dark, and then flung herself at me. "Dick!" she said. "Dick, oh my God! I thought you were dead." She clung to me, nuzzling with her face into the front of my jacket, but I took hold of her arms and pushed her very gently away from me. "It's not Dick," I said.

She jerked away from me as violently as she had flung herself at me. We stared into each other's faces, trying to pick out what we could in the darkness. Then she shook her head, very slowly. "I'm sorry," she said. "It was the voice. It's exactly the same. But you're only his brother."

"That's it," I said. "I'm only his brother."

We began to walk back toward the house, side by side in the tunnel of trees. The dark thing stayed where it was, standing there by the track. It was a stone of some sort. We said nothing to each other all the way back. The house was full of lights, and as we came round the end of it, she stopped and looked at me steadily in the glow from the uncurtained windows. She said, "You're very like him. It's not only the voice."

I said, "Miss Merrion said I was very different."

"Cynthia?" she said. "Cynthia didn't like him."

We came in at the front door together and Merrion came out of a sitting room on the left. He had a glass in his hand. He said, "Oh—I was going to introduce you, but I see you've already met. Ethel, this is Mr. Hawkins. My wife."

She said, "Yes, we've already met." She went on up the stairs.

Merrion looked after her for a moment. Then he turned back to me. "Well," he said, "come and have a drink."

CHAPTER 2

You would not have thought of Ethel Merrion as a small woman if it had not been for the contrast between her and her sister-in-law. This was violent, and the differences were not only physical. I put Cynthia at about five years younger than Merrion and Ethel at ten or more. I never knew Ethel's actual age, but I still think this would be about right. She was a woman of medium height with a nicely rounded figure. She had a pink and white complexion, brown hair and hazel eyes. She did everything with an impulsive, darting quickness which made her seem even younger than she was. But it was natural to her; there was nothing affected or kittenish about it. She was visibly on the defensive in that household, but she was nobody's fool. Her attraction was immediate and obvious. I knew why Merrion had married her, and I had a pretty good idea, even from the start, what Cynthia must have thought about it when he had.

Once he had made up his mind to it, Merrion was not a bad host. He had the academic's trick of maintaining a pleasant, easy relation without ever getting below a certain depth. His reserves were enormous, but he kept them well out of sight. My difficulty was to know who was my hostess. Even that difficulty fairly quickly became less important. The two women had got the thing worked out between them. There was a lot of intelligence all round. Provided you were up to it, it was a comfortable household on this carefully maintained superficial level. I think if I had been anyone but Dick's brother, I could have stayed on that level. Even as it was, I could have packed up his things and gone off next day if Ethel Merrion had not mistaken my voice for his. It was that that started it.

After dinner, at what seemed the appropriate moment, I said to Merrion, "Tell me about your abbey," but he smiled and shook his head.

"I can't," he said. "Not yet. I haven't had time to work on it. It needs a lot of work. It's going to be interesting."

"But I mean—what's its history?"

"It hasn't got any—not before 1850 or so. It was gone long before the Dissolution. That's one of the interesting things. There are others like it, of course. There are some we know only from aerial photographs. This one would have escaped even that—the trees cover everything. Only a chap called Braithwaite discovered it and bought it up."

"And built this house?"

He smiled at me, as if I was an undergraduate who had asked an intelligent question. "That's right. He was a Midland manufacturer. Plenty of money, of course. I suppose he fancied himself as the owner of an abbey. What we should now call a status symbol. He acquired a knighthood, too. An impressive pair of assets, by any standards. Sir Josiah Braithwaite, he called himself. He got the abbey marked on the survey sheet, but he didn't do anything about it. Just liked having it."

"At least he didn't dig it up and build his house in it—or with it."

"No." He was looking at me again, wondering what to say. "No," he said, "I think he thought this was near enough."

"But you're going to investigate it properly—excavate and so on? I gather—I ought to know, but I'm afraid I don't—I gather this is your particular speciality?"

"Why should you?" he said. "I am a medievalist, yes. And I have done a good deal of work on monastic sites. The idea is to give up my university job one of these days and settle down here and work at it whole time. It's a chance not many people get. An undisturbed site, you see?"

"And one no one else can get at first?"

He gave a small deprecating laugh. He sounded almost coy. "Well," he said, "there is that, I admit. I suppose like Sir Josiah I like owning an abbey. But I mean—it really does promise to be interesting. I don't know—I don't want to bore you with details."

I said, "You won't bore me." I really meant it. It was the man who interested me, of course, at that stage, not the abbey. But it did not seem necessary to explain this.

"Well," he said again. It was a trick of his, this. He would say, "Well—" and look at you, wondering all the time what he really wanted to say to you. "Well," he said, "it looks like a Cistercian site. The different orders used different plans, you know. And the Cistercians did come to these remote places. Anyway, it was pretty big. And then at some point, I think pretty early, it was destroyed. I rather think a lot of it was burnt. There was no rebuilding. The site was just abandoned, and the abbey disappeared from the records. And of course the trees grew over it. So there it was until Sir Josiah found it. It's—it's an unusual history."

I said, "Yes, I can see that." I looked at him and he looked at me. He still had this half-apologetic air, as if he was afraid of boring a layman. "Of course," I said, "this wasn't Dick's line at all, was it?"

"Dick?" he said. He sounded almost puzzled, as if he wondered for a moment who I was talking about. I was not going to explain. I just went on looking at him. "Oh no," he said, "your brother—Dick—was a prehistorian. He was—interested, of course. But his speciality was quite different."

"He was a man of wide interests," I said.

"Indeed, yes." He got up. "There'll be coffee," he said. "Shall we go and find some?"

I got up too. "I'd like that," I said. He went out into the hall and I went out after him. Only Cynthia was in the sitting room. She sat behind the coffee things, watching the two of us as we came in.

"I've been hearing about the abbey," I said.

She said, "You mustn't let Roger bore you. How do you like your coffee?"

"Black, please," I said, "with plenty of sugar. He won't, I assure you. I find it all very interesting." I took the cup she handed me. "I'll have a look at Dick's things tomorrow, shall I?"

"Yes," she said. "Do by all means. You know where they are."

"How long was he here, in fact?"

She was giving Merrion his coffee, and they looked at each other, wondering which of them was going to answer the question. Merrion said, "Oh, not long. A week or two, I suppose."

Cynthia took a breath, and I thought she was going to add something, but she thought better of it. "I met him last year," said Merrion. "He came to Bristol for some seminar or other. I told him about this place, and he said he'd like to come and see it and try some of the local climbs. So we fixed it up."

I said, "You have to be at Bristol during the term, I take it?"

"That's right. Ethel and I are mostly there and Cynthia holds the fort here. We get up here when we can, of course."

I said to Cynthia, "It must be lonely for you here on your own." I said this because it is the sort of thing one says. I did not really for a moment suppose Cynthia would be lonely anywhere, or would put up with it if she was. I was thinking I had much rather visit Llanglas during the university term, when only Cynthia was here. Dick of course would have had other views. I assumed he had met Ethel Merrion along with her husband at Bristol, and had come up here to try his hand at the local ascents. One at least of them I thought he had not expected to find, and probably had not found, particularly difficult. But one of the others, unexpectedly but finally, had beaten him. Poor old Dick. All the same, I fancied that right up to the last he had been enjoying himself.

All this time Cynthia and I were looking at each other over the coffee cups. It was not really very long, of course, but there was something very timeless in those wide gray eyes. She said, "I don't find it so. I am alone a lot, of course. But I like that. And then Roger comes up when he can. It's much better to keep the place open." She did not mention Ethel at all.

"It feels permanently lived in," I said. "Not at all like one of those week-end retreats that people are always going to retire to some time. There's no mistaking a second-class home."

Merrion said, "Bristol is my second-class home. I—" He looked at me, wondering how he ought to put it. "This is where I live," he said. He did not mention Ethel either.

"I think you're lucky," I said. "Even without the abbey. With the abbey, from what you say, you're very lucky indeed."

He said, "I'm very lucky, yes." He said it with a sudden absolute conviction. The hesitation, or the academic caution, or whatever it was, lifted completely for a moment, and the man's feelings showed almost unnervingly through the gap. Where your treasure is, I thought, there shall your heart be also. Most people have their treasures. I have met some odd ones in my time, but when a man mentions his, there is no mistaking it. I knew Merrion's. At least it was not Ethel. I wondered if Cynthia had one, and I found myself suddenly almost painfully eager to know what and where it was.

But there was nothing more to be said now. I got up. I said, "I wonder if you'll excuse me if I go to bed early? I've had a long drive, and your air here is strong stuff."

Cynthia said, "Of course," and we said our polite good-nights. I left them in the sitting room and went out into the hall, shutting the door behind me. There was no one about. I could hear no sounds from the kitchen, where I had heard, earlier, the voice of some local part-timer helping with the washing up. I wondered, of course, where Ethel Merrion was. I had no reason, even then, to think of her as the victim of a deliberate exclusion. I did not believe she thought of herself like that. She was independent. But if she had her difficulties, she would have to solve them for herself. I fancied that, here at least, she spent a good deal of time by herself, and I wondered where she spent it and what she did. Also, I saw how much the presence here of a man like Dick might have meant to her. Apart from his other qualifications, Dick was very intelligent and companionable, and she would be needing that. It might even be her chief need. I doubted whether the obvious view of the case was the right one. I went on upstairs.

There were lights on in the corridor. Once it was dark outside, the whole house was kept very well lit. It was one of the things you noticed. I went toward the door of my room and then, just before I got to it, stopped and opened the door of the room next to it. There was a light on and the curtains were closely drawn. Ethel Merrion was kneeling on the floor in the middle of the room. There was an open suitcase in front of her, and she had some small thing in her hands. As I opened the door, her head turned and she looked up at me over her shoulder. At the same time she put whatever she was holding back in the case and pulled the lid down over it. There was no mistaking the look on her face. She was startled, of course, but also she was frightened.

When she saw who it was, most of the fright went out of her face. Not only that; she made very little attempt to hide the fact that she had been frightened. She let out a long sigh of relief. Then she got to her feet, quite slowly, and turned and faced me. She said, "Shut the door."

I shut the door behind me without turning round. I did it, without thinking, as quietly as I could. She said, "I was just looking at Dick's things, I thought—I thought you might be taking them away soon, and I wanted to look at them. Do you mind?"

I said, "Of course I don't mind. Why should I?"

"I heard you coming, but I never thought you'd come in here. I didn't think you'd come up as soon as this."

"I was tired," I said, "and decided to go to bed early. I knew Dick's things were in here, but I didn't mean to come in here, not tonight. I'm sorry."

She came in very quickly on that. She had got over her shock, and her natural quickness was reasserting itself. "No, no," she said, "don't be sorry. There's no need to be. Do you want to look at them now?"

"I don't think so. Tomorrow will do. But please believe me—I didn't want to disturb you. I had no idea you were here. You can't see the light from outside."

She said, "I know that."

"Well—you stay here, if you like. I'll go to my room."

She shook her head violently. "No," she said, "not now. I must go." I stood aside and she went past me to the door. We both heard at the same moment somebody's feet coming up the stairs.

I have said she was quick in her ways, but I don't

think I have ever seen anyone make what must have been quite a complicated calculation and act on it so quickly. For a split second she stood there listening. Then she turned again, went past me almost without looking at me and stepped behind the drawn curtains of the window. She was in there and the curtains had stopped moving almost before I knew what she was at. I do not know whether I am a natural intriguer. I had never thought of myself as one. I think some of her speed and urgency must have communicated itself to me. I went back to the middle of the room, opened the suitcase and knelt by it exactly as she had been kneeling. I put my hands into it and lifted out a jacket folded on top. I wished, afterward, that I had looked to see what it was she had put back so hurriedly, but my mind was not working as fast as that. I had got the jacket out and was looking at the things underneath when the door opened behind me. I turned, with an enormous and wholly assumed deliberation, but I already knew who it was. Merrion had his head round the door. His face already wore an expression of unobtrusive but sympathetic interest. He said, "Oh, I'm sorry. Having a look at your brother's things?"

I put the jacket back, shut down the lid of the case and snapped the locks shut. Then I got to my feet. I did it all very slowly. "Yes," I said, "but I didn't really mean to do it now. I just turned in on an impulse, to see what there was of it. But I see it's all packed up. I'll have a proper look at it tomorrow."

I went toward the door and he stepped back into the corridor. I went out after him. I switched the light off as I went and shut the door behind me. We stood there, outside the shut door in the brightly lit corridor, looking at each other. I said, "If you're not too busy, I wonder if you'd show me the abbey tomorrow? I'd like to see it before I go." I made no move toward the door of my room.

"Of course," he said. "You do understand, there's precious little to see? Mostly mounds with the rubble under them. Just the outline of the thing, really. As I say, it all needs opening up, and it's going to be a long job."

"All the same, I'd like to have it explained. It's new to me, a thing like this."

He said, "I'll do that, with pleasure." I still did not move. "Well—" he said. This time the pause was longer than ever. "Well, I'll say good-night again. I hope I didn't disturb you. Have a look at your brother's things tomorrow, and then when you're ready we'll do a walk over the site." He nodded and went off along the corridor and down the stairs. I watched him until he disappeared and then listened to his feet going down the stairs and across the hall. A door opened and shut, but I could not tell which. I went into my room, shutting the door with slightly unnecessary force. After that I listened for quite a while, but I never heard a sound from next door.

I knew finally that Ethel Merrion must have gone, because there was no reason why she should want to stay and there had been nothing to prevent her going. No one else had come upstairs. I got undressed and went across to the bathroom. My drowsiness had gone and I was wide awake now. I lay soaking in the hot water, wondering about Mr. and Mrs. Merrion as a couple. Speculating about the relation between a husband and wife is one of the most unprofitable occupations, but you still do it. I did not at the end of it know what Merrion felt about his wife, but I knew that in some way he minded about her. I knew that she was left very much to her own life, but I did not think, even so, that she was free. I knew where Dick came into it, in one way at least. But I could not help wondering whether there might be other ways. I got no further than that. I was sleepy again now. I heaved myself out of the bath and went across to my room.

CHAPTER 3

I HAVE HEARD it said that every man has among his personal possessions something that he would rather not have found after his death. I thought that this was probably less likely to be true of Dick than of most people. He was not a man for private pleasures and commitments. Nevertheless, to go through anyone's things when he is not there to permit it is a slightly unnerving experience. I suppose if you are a detective or a criminal it is different: the owner of the things is the enemy, and you hope to be cleverer than he is. When he was your younger brother, and is now dead, the urge to apologize, however innocent your intentions, is very strong.

The curtains were still drawn when I went into the room. There was not much daylight outside to start with, and it made the room very dark. I switched on the light and walked across to the window. I knew there was no one behind the curtains now. All the same, I hesitated just for a moment before I opened them and threw them back. There was, of course, no one there. All I saw was the bare hillside, mostly green but already ribbed with rock, running up steeply from very close beside the house. The skyline was so high that I had to go close to the window and peer upward to see it. For a climber, I suppose, it was a summons and a challenge, but I found it oppressive. Even with the curtains drawn back, the room was still too dark.

I knelt in front of the suitcase on the floor, as Ethel Merrion and I had both knelt the night before. There was another suitcase, shut, under the bed. They had all sorts of mountainous and exotic labels on them. Dick was not a man to make a thing of exotic labels on his cases, but he was not a man to take them off, either. He would not mind a little mild exhibitionism, even if he did not need it. But the things inside the cases were very ordinary. Also, it occurred to me, even as I opened the case, that it was not Dick who had packed it. Someone had collected his things from wherever they were distributed about the room, and had folded them and packed them neatly away. I had no doubt at all that it was Cynthia. It would be, anyway, and there was something about the way the cases were packed that showed her hand. I was glad of this, though it did not occur to me to wonder why.

As I say, it was all very ordinary. There was a certain amount of the heavy stuff he would wear for climbing, though no doubt one complete set of climbing gear had disappeared with him. The rest was a mixture of town and country stuff, all to my mind fairly elegant and expensive, but no more than I should have expected. The stuff he used for washing and shaving and doing his hair was all severely plain. The only very personal thing I found was the medal, and that was at the bottom of the first case. Perhaps I should call it a medallion. At any rate, I knew what it was. I had seen it before, though not for years. It was a plain steel disc that had been given to members by a climbing club Dick belonged to when he was a boy. You had to complete a particular climb to the satisfaction of the committee. Then you got your medal and were admitted a full member. Dick had got his when he was sixteen or seventeen, and had been enormously proud of it. I remembered him bringing it home in triumph and showing it to all the family. I do not think I had seen it since, but now here it was again, slung on a leather lace greasy with being worn next to the skin. There was something extraordinarily pathetic about it, seen suddenly in these circumstances and after all this time. The truth is, I had liked Dick better as a boy than I liked him later, and here was the young Dick again, still carried secretly under the elegant trappings of the grown-up. It was a little too symbolic for comfort. I dropped the medal into the case again and put the other things back on top. There was nothing to see and nothing to decide. It was all perfectly good stuff, only I had still no idea what should be done with it now Dick was dead.

When I went downstairs, I found Merrion in the sitting room with the day's paper. He lowered the paper and looked up at me and said, "Well?" This time it was definitely interrogative, but it was as noncommittal as ever. It occurred to me that if I had come down expecting to be shown over the abbey site, there he was waiting for me, as good as gold, but if I had changed my mind or forgotten about it, he was not going to remind me. I had not forgotten about it, and I had not changed my mind. But first I said, "I've been through Dick's things. It's all quite good stuff. I suppose—I suppose it has a cash value of some sort. Only in a case like this, when death can't be presumed, I'm not sure what the proper procedure is. Anyway, you don't want it in the house. If you agree, I suggest I take it with me when I go. Then I'll get advice on what's to be done with it."

"Yes," he said, "yes, of course. If it won't be a nuisance to you."

"None at all," I said. "I'll do that, then." I had sat down opposite him, and now I sat there looking at him, waiting to see whether he would make the next move. He held out for a remarkably long time. Then he said,

"Well—" and I looked at him more expectantly than ever.

"Well," he said, "I don't know if you'd like to—"

He hung up again, but this time I could not be bothered to push the thing any further. "You promised to show me the abbey site," I said.

He was all alacrity at once. "Of course," he said, "we can go now if you're ready."

I said, "I'm ready," and we both got up.

"Good," he said. "It won't take us long just to walk over. I don't know—" he looked at me again, sideways, as we went out, "I don't know how far you share your brother's archaeological interests."

"Hardly at all. In any case, as you know, his special interest was the neolithic. I've talked to him sometimes about some of the engineering problems of megalith building. He used to try his ideas on me about how the stones might have been handled. But that's hardly relevant here."

"No, indeed. Perhaps you might help me in the opposite way. I mean—you might perhaps have some idea of what brought the abbey down. But I'm afraid there isn't much to go on."

"I doubt it," I said. "Anyway, let's see what there is."

It was a gray morning when we went outside. There was unbroken cloud driving eastward over the mountains, and even down here there was enough wind to keep the tops of the trees continuously moving. The oaks were turning yellow but still in full leaf, and the noise they made formed a stealthy background to everything we said. I did not like the place any more at this time of the morning than I had the evening before. Once we were under the trees, I could not even see very much more. It was not only in the dark that the wood looked thickly grown. The green-rutted track lay straight ahead, but most of the time I do not think I could see more than seven or eight yards on either side.

I mean at ground level, where the thorny undergrowth filled all the gaps between the boles. Higher up you could see into the arched vaults under the treetops. They were full of the intermittent glimmer that came down through the shifting leaves, and looked enormous.

Merrion said, "There was just this one approach road. There are ways up into the hills in one or two places, but they aren't much more than sheep tracks. But you've already been this way, perhaps?"

"Not far. I started walking along the track last night, but it was getting pretty dark. Then I met your wife and came back with her."

"Yes. Well, as I say, this was the only road in. It is continuous, of course, with the road on the other side of the house. Sir Josiah built his house right across it."

"He didn't want intruders, either," I said.

He turned and looked at me for a moment. "No?" he said. "No, I suppose not."

"All the same," I said, "someone has kept the road open. I mean—the trees haven't grown over it, have they?"

"That is so. I haven't done any digging on it, but I think there must be a good deal of metal underneath."

I said, "That wouldn't stop the oaks, not once they'd been allowed to get their roots down. What about the site of the abbey itself?"

"It's pretty thickly grown," he said. "You'll see. There are open spaces, of course."

I nodded, but did not pursue the matter. The hump in the road, which I had noticed in the darkness, was not so apparent even in this amount of daylight, but I could see the shoulders of earth banks under the trees on both sides of us. I stopped and looked at them. "Some sort of a wall," I said.

"That's right," Merrion said. He went on walking and I followed him. "A perimeter wall, apparently. One of the characteristics of Cistercian sites. They liked building out in the wilds, but they put a wall round themselves for protection."

I thought about this. "If the abbey was in the middle of the wood and the thing is symmetrical," I said, "the enclosed area must be very big,"

"It is. Quite exceptionally big. At Fountains the wall encloses ninety acres, but this will be a good deal more. As I say, the whole layout is exceptional."

I had forgotten the single stone pillar standing by the track, and even in this light it came as a shock to me. It was the only straight man-made thing and in that world of shifting leaves and shifting light the only thing that was absolutely motionless. No wonder it had scared me in the dark. It was not in fact in the middle of the track. It stood to one side, and on the side nearest to the track I could see a slight projection, like the corbel at the springing point of an arch. It looked like the last remnant of a gateway that had once spanned and blocked the road. When we got nearer to it, I could see that it was squared up to form a rectangular pier, and that a line of blurred molding ran horizontally across it at the level of the corbel. It was on Merrion's side of the track, and he was slightly ahead of me, so that he got to it before I did.

He made a sudden small sound. It was not the sort of sound I expected to hear from him. I was not sure whether it was exasperation or real upset. He darted forward, reached up a hand and pulled something down from the far side of the corbel. He bundled it up and pushed it into his jacket pocket. I got no more than a glimpse of it, but I thought I knew what it was. It was a daisy chain, or something like it, a thin single garland of small white flowers. He turned and looked at me. His mouth smiled, but his face was full of an enormous distaste. He knew I must have seen it. "Children," he said. He still looked at me, wondering what more to say. He said, "They know they're not supposed to come in here. It's very annoying."

He walked on again, and I walked after him. I said, "Yes. I don't imagine, in fact, there's much harm they can do."

He shook his head at that. He seemed agitated out of all proportion to the facts. "You can't tell," he said, "you can't tell. I don't want anything disturbed at all."

I said, "No, of course not." I found myself soothing him, as if he was a child himself. I still did not know what it was all about. Some time later the trees fell back on the left and I saw, running parallel with the track, a long green mound with the vestiges of very old masonry just showing along its crest. Merrion went on, almost hurrying, until ahead of us the green shimmer turned to a steady gray daylight, and for the first time we saw a long strip of sky between the tops of the trees. Then at last he turned off the track and made for the end of the clearing. There were stones everywhere now. They lay in tumbled lines, just keeping their heads out of the engulfing green. Merrion stopped, and I stopped beside him. "Well—" he said.

The wind rustled and whispered in the trees and the clouds still rolled continuously overhead. We stood there, looking at the desolation of the place.

"This was the church," he said. "This long space running east and west. Long and narrow, like nearly all the Cistercian churches. They were austere people, the white monks. They didn't go in much for processions, and they didn't encourage pilgrims. Not that this would have been here long enough to become a place of pilgrimage."

I stared at it, suddenly and unexpectedly appalled. "Not one stone left upon another," I said. "I wonder what they'd done to call down the wrath of God on this scale. Could there have been an earthquake in these parts?"

Merrion turned and looked at me. His face was pale and his mouth drawn hard down at the corners, but his eyes shone. I thought, he likes it like this. Something in this destruction appeals to him. Then the lids came down over his eyes and he shook his head. "No earthquakes," he said. "Or so I am told. The wrath of God, as you say, it may have been. It is curious that you should say that. I have thought the same thing myself. Destruction it must have been. It was not, you see, pillaged for stone, like the great churches pulled down at the Dissolution. It was just pulled down. There was fire, too, I think. I can show you the traces of black earth and burnt stones." He walked forward into the end of the open space and I walked after him. It was a relief, even under that threatening sky, to be clear of the trees. "What's more," he said, "I fancy the brothers perished with their abbey. Or some of them, anyhow. There are bones, even now, under the rubble. Whatever they had done, something caught up with them."

He turned and put on his academic manner, as visibly as if he was hitching his gown on to his shoulders. "The cloisters would have been there," he said, "next to the church on the south side. As I say, their central layout at least was very standardized. And it's all here, you see, that's the point. It's all here to be dug out. It's only the scale and the detail that's in doubt. He turned again and went back under the edge of the trees. "I can show you some of the main outlines, if you're interested."

I said, "I don't know. I'm not sure, really, that I am. Will you bear with me? To tell you the truth, I find the whole thing a bit oppressive."

He took me up quickly on that. "Of course," he said. "I know how you feel, and it's not your job, after all. Let's go back, then." We found our way back to the track and set our faces eastward. For quite a long time we walked in silence. Presently he said, "You think it's queer wanting to own a place like this. But it's all a very long time ago, you know. Destruction is one of the processes of history."

"Of course," I said. "In any case, I think I prefer the wrath of God to the greed of the king's men. One doesn't have to be angry about it."

"Indeed, no," he said.

When we came to the solitary pillar, I said, "That's a monolith, isn't it? That must be unusual, surely?"

He flicked his eyes sideways at me, but kept on walking. "Unusual," he said, "certainly. But it does occur. The local stone falls naturally into these long sections."

I let it go at that. All the same, I thought I should like to have another look at the thing when Merrion was not there. And I wondered. I wondered how far away the nearest children lived. I wondered how many children in this sophisticated age still played with daisy chains and why in God's name they should want to do it in a place like this. I wondered what Ethel Merrion had been doing at the foot of the stone in near darkness, and why, even in the darkness and whatever my voice was like, she had been able to persuade herself for a moment that someone was walking to meet her whom she believed dead.

CHAPTER 4

Cynthia said, "But there's no need for you to go at once. I mean, unless you've got something else you ought to be doing. You've come a long way."

She spoke, as she looked, very direct. Her eyes held mine steadily and as a matter of course. I do not think there was any challenge in them, but there was very little evasion. I thought how shattering it would be to be in love with a woman like this. There is so much play-acting in nearly all love, but with her it would not do. When the thing finally went on the rocks, there would be precious little saved from the wreck. I assumed that it would go on the rocks sooner or later, because in my experience it always did. If I had thought about it, I should have seen that a love which did not go on the rocks would be the most shattering thing of all, but the possibility did not really occur to me. I said, "When does your brother have to be back at Bristol?"

I was not sure how far this was really relevant, but it was something I wanted to know. Being the person she was, she jumped the irrelevance and went to what was in my mind. She said, "You'd be happier here without him?" As usual, neither of us mentioned Mrs. Merrion.

"That would be up to you," I said, "obviously. Speaking purely for myself, yes, I think I should."

She nodded. "You don't find him easy?"

"I think I find him easy to get on with but uneasy in himself."

"Yes." She looked away from me then, because it was not me she was thinking about. She stared at the gray daylight outside the window. Then she turned to me again. She said, "You're much more intelligent than your brother, aren't you?"

She said it quite seriously, but I smiled at her. "He was always the bright one of the family," I said.

"Oh, that of course," she said. "I don't mean that."

I said, "Did he get on with your brother all right? I don't see they had much in common. Not even their professional interests, or only marginally." I knew, of course, one interest they had shared, but I did not think it necessary to say so. She would know it as well as I did, but she had no reason, yet, to think I knew it at all.

She said, "Roger invited him here, and seemed glad enough to have him. I hadn't met him, of course, before he came."

"But when he came, you didn't particularly like him?"

"I didn't really see very much of him or get to know him particularly well. I admit I didn't find very much to like in him. But he was your brother, and he's dead. Can't we leave it at that? I don't think you were very fond of him yourself?"

"I think I was a little jealous of him."

"You?" she said. "What had you to be jealous of?"

I smiled at her, but I felt immensely serious. I was not used to being taken seriously. "The usual thing, surely," I said. "He was the younger brother, but the more successful. He did a lot of things better than I did. He always seemed to get what he wanted."

She said, "But not what you wanted."

I thought about this. "No," I said, "perhaps not. But then I didn't often seem to get what I wanted, either. I still don't."

"You want more," she said. I looked at her, and she looked at me, and I knew, with a sudden and frightening certainty, that this was true. I knew, or thought I knew, what Dick had wanted here, and I knew already what I wanted, and I wanted much more than he had. I suppose something must have showed in my face, because she dropped her eyes and turned away, and I could not remember seeing her do this before.

I said, "You haven't in fact answered my question."

"Roger? He'll be going back in about a fortnight."

"And Ethel will go with him?"

This seemed to surprise her. She said, "Oh yes," but she looked at me, frowning slightly, as if something had been left unexplained.

"I'm sorry," I said. "I wasn't sure. I thought perhaps—"

She shook her head, slowly and with a curious emphasis. "They're inseparable," she said. She hesitated, as if that was not quite what she wanted to say. Then she said, "He won't let her out of his sight."

I could see the danger signals, but I wanted the thing explained. "But he does," I said. "I haven't been here long, I admit, but I've hardly seen them together. I mean, except at meals and so on."

"Here?" she said. "This is a small place, after all. We're all pretty well on top of each other anyhow." She got up and went to the door. Then she turned and faced me again. She said suddenly and harshly, "They're very much man and wife, you know." She turned again and went out.

I sat there for what must have been quite a time, staring at the shut door and trying to sort out the deep undercurrent of exhilaration in my mind from the curiously shocking nastiness left floating on its surface. There was no mistaking the nastiness, but I could not see where it came from. I did not for a moment believe that it was in Cynthia herself. The trite bitterness of the devoted sister against her brother's wife was not for her. She was too good for that. Nor did I believe, despite the facts as I took them to be, that the nastiness lay in Ethel Merrion. Whatever your mind told you about Ethel, she left a sweet taste in the mouth. That left Merrion himself, or Dick, who had been my brother and was now dead. Dick was never nasty. A little bit of a lightweight, but with no nastiness in him. So it came down to Merrion, in whom the waters ran deep and might hide anything.

I got up and wandered to the window. I was more deeply disturbed than I had been for a very long time. I wanted to take Dick's suitcases and go, but I knew I could not, not now. There was too much here that I wanted to know, and too much that I wanted, quite simply, to possess. I could of course go now and come back when Merrion and his wife had gone, but this seemed disingenuous and even slightly comic, and I was unwilling to let myself appear in that light. So for the moment I would stay, but I did not know for how long or what would come of it if I did.

My eyes flicked sideways at the first sign of movement, and I watched the man move right across my field of vision, until he disappeared behind the buildings at the back of the house. He was enormously tall. His clothes flapped round him in the wind, but I got the impression that he was very thin under them, and his head looked disproportionately small. He was too much like a walking scarecrow for comfort. He walked very deliberately, pouncing forward slightly on the front of his feet. There was nothing stealthy about him at all. When he was halfway across, he turned and looked at the side of the house. I did not know whether he saw me watching him, or whether anyone else was watching him from another window, but in either case he was not going to let it worry him. On the contrary, I was fairly certain that he wanted to be seen. He allowed himself no more than one quick glance at the house, and then stalked on, with his head thrust forward a little, self-consciously bent on whatever he thought he was doing. He was an extraordinary figure.

After he had gone, I stood there for a moment, wondering what in the world to make of him. Then I heard movements in the house behind me, and I had turned round, but was still by the window, when the door of the room opened and Merrion put his head in. It was the second time I had seen him do this, and it occurred to me that it was very characteristic of him. He felt his way into a room just as he felt his way into a conversation. He looked at me, taking in my position and calculating its probable consequences. Then he summoned up his quick, uneasy smile and said, "Did you see our visitant?"

It must have been the word he used, coupled with the effect the place was having on me, but I found myself saying, perfectly seriously, "Was it a ghost?"

He shook his head. "No, no," he said, "flesh and blood. Though not much flesh, in fact. That was old Evans maintaining his right of way."

I said, "Ah, that explains it."

He looked at me with a touch of anxiety. "Explains what?" he said.

"His manner. The way he walked. I thought he was maintaining something."

The anxiety faded and he smiled again. "I know," he said, "I know exactly. The look of conscious defiance. I don't know why he should be defiant. I have never tried to stop him."

"You own the house," I said. "The house stops him. I bet he'd walk through the middle of it if he could. As it is, he has to go round. But he doesn't like doing it."

He said, "You have a very vivid imagination for a man of your profession."

There was a distinct touch of acid there, and I hastened to disarm him. I smiled cheerfully. I did not feel cheerful. I never did with Merrion. But I smiled as cheerfully as I could. "Not really," I said. "You mentioned the right of way, after all. And we had already agreed that Sir Josiah built his house across the old road. And I know what these quiet places are like. An affront like that takes more than a couple of generations to work itself out. I see old Evans as the last protester. Am I wrong?"

"On the contrary, you are exactly right. Your mind works very quickly."

I had been commended for my intelligence twice in one morning, and was beginning to have a better conceit of myself. I thought what extraordinary people these were. But it was only in Merrion that I resented it. I said, "And what, having made his gesture of defiance, does he do? Turn round and walk back?"

He hesitated a bit. Then he said, "Pretty well. He'll walk—I don't know, some way into the wood, I think. Then, as you say, he'll come back. He's an eccentric character, by ordinary standards."

"So I should imagine. But I mean—a right of way is a right of way to somewhere. Otherwise it wouldn't be claimed as a right. Where is old Evans going?"

Merrion looked at me blankly. "There isn't a right of way," he said. "Or if there was, it was extinguished long ago. I have the deeds, after all. The village people may have had rights in the wood once. There were several sorts they could have had. Probably by Sir Josiah's time all they did was gather firewood, and they don't even want that now. But as you say, these things die hard. I've never seen old Evans take anything out of the wood. I think it's just that he's always walked there and isn't going to be stopped now. The house was empty, of course, for some time before I bought it. Whether he used to come then I don't know. It's not much fun protesting if there's no one to protest to. Since I've been here, he's kept it up pretty regularly. And as I say, I've never stopped him."

I said, "Perhaps if you go on not stopping him, he'll give up protesting."

"It's possible," he said. He was tired of the subject now. He had said what he had come in to say, and now he was looking for a way to let himself out again. I made it as easy for him as I could. I had no wish to keep him.

"I thought I'd walk into the village," I said. "Is there anywhere I can buy myself some tobacco?"

"Oh yes, indeed. The shop has a license. I don't know if they'll have much choice."

"I'm not fussy," I said. "They'll have something I can use." I moved toward the door. He was still only just inside it.

"Good," he said. "I'll see you later, then." He slipped out ahead of me, and by the time I came out into the hall the door of his working room was shut. I took a mackintosh in case, and went out into the gray weather.

I had in fact been perfectly honest with Merrion. I needed tobacco and I needed a walk, and had made up my mind to get the two together. It was no doubt because I had had no other thought in my head that Merrion had not looked for one. I reckoned he would be as quick to spot an ulterior motive as most people. But now that I was away on my walk to the village, it occurred to me that I might well at some point meet old Evans and get a closer look at him. He had presumably come from the village and would be returning to it. I was going to the village and should be returning from it. Unless it took him much longer to do whatever he had to do in the wood than it took me to buy my tobacco, we ought to meet somewhere. I wanted to meet him. Apart from anything else, he was a human curiosity in his own right. But also, I wanted to know how far Merrion's account of him was true, and why he had found it necessary to give me any account of him at all.

I thought if a stray cat had crossed the grass beside the house, Merrion would not have come into the sitting room to find out if I had seen it, and then, if he found I had, told me what it was up to. I wondered what there was about old Evans, if Merrion's account of him was true, which made him that much more important than a stray cat. Not that I should necessarily be any nearer knowing, even if I did meet him. But I thought it would be worth a try.

I was surprised to find, as I went down the road, how suddenly the hills fell away from both sides of it and let you out into the level country to the east, where the village and the main road were. You cannot get the feel and shape of a country from inside a closed car, or not as you can when you are on your feet and in the open. Coming in, I had simply followed the road, aware of steep hillsides on either hand. Now it was like going out of a door. I had a sudden, eccentric picture of Merrion, when he had come there for the first time, putting his head in through the gap in the hills and looking at Llanglas doubtfully before he had made up his mind to go in any further. But then he had no doubt come in a car, too. I walked on, conscious suddenly of a lightening of the atmosphere. There was space here for the air to move in between me and the clouds. Even when I came to the village, I should not be subjected to the same perpetual mental scrutiny, and I was less likely to be awarded occasional prizes for my intelligence. Indeed, if I knew anything about villages, this was very unlikely indeed.

In this at least I was right. From the moment I got inside the shop, I was flooded with information. I was told the virtues and drawbacks of every kind of tobacco in stock in fluent, persuasive and lilting English. I had in fact smoked most of them at one time or another, but if I had been a boy buying his first pipeful, I could not have been better or more fully instructed. I was told about the brands which they might have been expected to stock, but did not, and why they stocked the brands they did, and who smoked them, and what they had said about them. I was told what my own probable reactions would be to the brand I finally chose. I was told, moving into a wider field, of the state of business and the state of the weather and of the road south as far as Cardiff. I was bidden a very kind good-bye, and walked out of the shop feeling a new man. I met old Evans suddenly at a bend in the road right in the gap of the hills.

Even though I was expecting it, his appearance at close range still startled me. On top of that flapping beanpole the face was chalk-white, but the eyes in the white face were as dark and bright as a monkey's. He was wearing an old beret pulled down tight on his head. I should not have put it past him to have a shock of white hair, but if he had, it was not visible. He knew who I was just as much as I knew him. He stared at me as we came up to each other, and then suddenly his whole face was contorted in an enormous, impish smile. The effect was extraordinarily unnerving. I never doubted that the man was to some extent a charlatan, but I had an uneasy feeling that his charlatanry did not go all the way down. Somewhere under it, apprehended through it as if through a distorting glass, some formidable quality remained.

He said, "Mr. Hawkins, is it, the brother of him that died?"

I do not know why I said it, because the idea had not at any point consciously entered my head, but I said, "We don't know he's dead."

He shook his head at me. He was no longer smiling. He must have been all of a head taller than I was. He stood there in the road, looking down at me, quite motionless, while the wind came from behind through the gap in the hills and blew his clothes about. "Dead he is," he said, "dead, and will never be found. Called back he's been, time and time over, but he's not come." His speech was almost a chant. It was a little ridiculous, but also a little horrifying.

I said, "Who's been calling him, then, Mr. Evans?" I put the question perfectly seriously, as you do to a professional fortuneteller. He may or may not have the right answers, but for the moment you take him at his own valuation. Otherwise it is no good asking him.

He smiled again, but only slightly. It was as if he found my question rather silly. "Those that want him back," he said. "It would not be anyone else."

I nodded but did not say anything. He looked at me for a moment or two. Then he lifted his hand and went on past me. I went on too, with the hills towering on both sides of me, watching at each bend of the road for the sight of the house against its dark background of trees. I wanted to speak to Ethel Merrion.

CHAPTER 5

By the time I came to the house I had changed my mind. I still wanted to speak to Ethel Merrion, but first I thought I would walk on into the wood, as Mr. Evans had walked, and see if I could get some idea what the old scarecrow did there. But I thought I would walk, not, like him, round the south side of the house, but round the north side. I was already consciously playing hide and seek with Merrion in this, but the game was of his choosing, not mine. For all I knew, I might be seen going round the north side by Cynthia or Ethel Merrion, or indeed by Merrion himself if he was no longer in his working room. But the idea of tiptoeing past in old Evans's footsteps was too blatant for me in my present state of mind. Practically, there was nothing in it either way. The line of the old road lay under the center of the house and the detour involved was the same. If it was a conscious evasion, it was one that would not need explaining.

I turned right when I got inside the gate. I walked with the steady, casual rhythm of a man walking mainly for the stake of walking. The north-facing windows of the house went past me on my left hand, but I did not turn my head and look at them as old Evans had done on the other side of the house. If anyone was watching me, defiance was the last thing I wanted to suggest.

I do not know if anyone watched me or not. If they did, they kept it to themselves. No one came pattering after me. If it had not turned out as it did, no one would have known that I had been in the wood at all. Even as it was, no one knew, then, what I had found there. When I got round the outbuildings and had picked up the green track on the far side, I actually waited a little to see if anyone followed me. The outbuildings screened me from the back of the house here, and no one could see me waiting. But no one came. I turned and went in under the trees. There was no need to pretend now, and I walked faster. I knew what I was making for, and I went straight to it.

I did not like having my feelings played on like this, and I went with a carefully neutral mind, daring the stone to shock me if it could. It did, still. I expect the psychologists would have plenty to say on the subject, especially the Freudians. The fact remains that nothing can defeat the impressiveness of the solitary standing stone pillar except the ludicrous trick of putting a human statue on top. I am not an expert in this field, but I feel fairly certain that that must have been a Roman invention. The Romans could spoil anything. But here there were no human distractions, just the great gray stone standing motionless with the trees whispering over it. I did not know what it could do to me, but I went up to it cautiously, as if there was danger in it.

It did not do anything. It just stood there. It must have been all of twelve feet high. It was weathered and in places lichened, but the edges were straight and vertical, and the sides laid off against each other at accurate right angles. Only the natural grain of the stone slanted slightly to the right, and it was on the right side, as I came up to it, that the corbel stood out from the face of the pillar. I wondered whether the whole stone had not originally leant a bit to the right, and then been trimmed to a vertical, and the corbel cut out of the unwanted stone at the top. I could not see why this should be so, but the corbel was in one piece with the pillar, and it had to come from somewhere. Also I wondered why, apart from its sheer size and solidity, the pillar had escaped the apparently deliberate destruction which seemed to have overtaken the rest of the abbey. The second pillar, which must have stood on the other side of the track, and the arch which must have sprung from the corbel, had gone altogether. I thought they had probably been built of ordinary masonry, and their dismembered stones would be somewhere under the green hummocks at the side of the track. Only this one pillar had remained, massive, monolithic and apparently indestructible.

The line of carved molding, which ran horizontally across the eastern face of the stone at the level of the corbel, was still well defined. It was simple, early stuff, presumably romanesque, though I did not know enough to identify or date it. The other three sides were rough and weathered, but apparently blank. I walked round the stone, looking up at it. The turf under my feet was hard and completely smooth, like the turf of a sheep track. I had the idea that a lot of other people had walked on it before me, perhaps old Evans within the last hour or two, certainly Ethel Merrion a couple of evenings ago. It was only just as I was leaving the stone that I saw the markings high up on the western face, and then I turned back for a closer look at them.

They were pretty faint. Most of them had been only lightly incised in the stone to start with, and time and the weather had blurred them a lot. But the lines were straight, and the pattern had some sort of deliberate unity. It was human work all right. I leant sideways, so that the intermittent light from overhead struck across the marks. I know I gasped, because I was conscious afterward of the sound I had made. I was looking at a human figure, a matchstick man sketched in in single strokes, but still horribly alive. It danced on the stone, holding its matchstick arms over its head and kicking its legs outward, and its enormous penis, half as long as its legs, stood up stiffly in front of it. It was obscenely jovial and surprisingly sophisticated. It was old, of course, but not really primitive. Whoever had done it had known what he was up to.

It was when I saw what he had done that I was really shaken. When you looked at it carefully, you saw that there had been two stages, and certainly two hands at work. Someone, a very long time ago, had cut a simple cross on the stone, the cross of the crucifix, with its lower arm longer than the others. Later, God knows how much later, but still a long time ago, someone else had taken a second, narrower chisel to it, and had transformed the cross into this gay little ithyphallic manikin. To call it sophisticated did not really meet the case. It was consciously and deliberately devilish.

I knew at once who had done it. It was the hand, or one of the hands, which had destroyed the abbey. It had to be. Of the abbey not one stone had been left upon another, but this one stone, for reasons I did not understand, still stood single and upright. The monks had christened it, and the destroyers, though they left it standing, had unchristened it. They had pulled down the abbey and gone back into the trees, leaving an overseer of their desolation, capering obscenely with his huge up-ended tool on the pillar of the doorway of the house of God.

The frightening thing was that even now the excitement was infectious. I was conscious of it, standing there dry-mouthed under the stone. The civilized top of my mind recoiled from the destruction of the abbey, but underneath it an older self was ready to join the dance. And I was not the only one. There was no place here for Merrion's children with their daisy chains. Someone hung their chaplet of flowers on the corbel, because there was nowhere else to hang it. But it was not, in their minds, the corbel they hung it on. I backed away from the stone, as I had come up to it, cautiously, as a priest backs away from the altar or a courtier from the person of royalty. Reverence is a rationalization. Deep down, and from a long way back, he is afraid to turn his back on what he knows is there.

I did turn, of course, after a few paces. Then I started walking back to the house. I walked slowly, with my eyes on the ground, so that I passed without really noticing them the two green banks which, some way along, crept up under the cover of the trees to either side of the track. I noticed them later. Now I had other things on my mind. It was because my eyes were on the ground that I did not see Ethel Merrion until I was almost alongside her.

She was standing dead still among the trees at the side of the track, watching me as I came along it. I do not think I could have passed her without seeing her, however much I was sunk in my own mind. I believe if I had, she would have let me go, but she was still too close to the track for that. My head came up with a jerk, and for a moment we stared into each other's eyes, both startled and both, for whatever different reasons, unequal to the meeting which we could not avoid.

I do not know how much my face revealed, but she had none of her husband's powers of concealment. I do not think she even had the instinct for it. She said, "How long have you been out here? I thought you'd gone to the village."

"I did," I said. "I came this way when I got back."

"Did you see old Evans?"

"Not here. Halfway back to the village."

She nodded. She seemed relieved for the moment. Then she said, "Did he speak to you?"

"Yes. Not much. He knew who I was."

"He would," she said. "There's not much he doesn't know. Did he mention Dick?"

"Only—" I hesitated, picking my words with care. "He only said that I must be Dick's brother and that Dick was dead."

"He said Dick was dead?"

"Oh yes. Why shouldn't he? Don't you think he is?"

She came out from between the trees and stood beside me on the track. "Yes," she said. "Yes, I think he's dead. The other evening—it was your voice, you see, coming suddenly like that when I couldn't see who it was. But I didn't really think—" She threw out her hands suddenly, and started to walk back toward the house. It was as if she was throwing away the last of her hope. "I know he's dead," she said.

I suppose it is rather a shocking thing to say, but Dick's death suddenly hit me hard for the first time. It was the utter desolation in Ethel Merrion's voice. Her face was turned away from me and I could not see it. I cannot say I saw Dick with her eyes, but at least for the moment I stopped seeing him with my own. I saw him simply as a person in the world, a cheerful, intelligent, exciting person, who on any reckoning left a gap and whose death was a sad waste. I put out a hand and took Ethel's arm, lightly, as she walked beside me. "I'm sorry," I said.

She turned her head and looked up at me. Her face was very white and woebegone, and as she turned her face up, a single small tear overflowed from one eye and rolled down her cheek. "You?" she said.

I said, "Why not me? You're the one who's hurt. He was only my brother."

She reached her other hand up and patted my hand where it rested on her arm. "Thank you," she said. "You're kind. I don't think Dick was, very. But it doesn't matter now."

"His death matters," I said.

She stopped and turned to face me. My hand came off her arm and we stood there, very close to each other but not touching. She said, "I wondered when you'd see that. But I think it's for me to say."

Her mouth no longer drooped. It was set now, and her face curiously hard. I was reminded at once of that tough, independent quality in her which I had noticed at first and then rather lost sight of. "For me," she said. "Do you see? It is for me to say how much Dick's death mattered. Not for you at all."

I stood there, looking down at her. I was suddenly very unhappy. I think she saw this, because her face softened and her eyes widened as she looked up at me. It was as if she was asking me for something, but I did not know what it was she wanted. "Please," she said.

Whatever it was she wanted, I could not at that moment have refused it. "All right," I said. "Whatever you say. Only try not to let it hurt you too much."

She turned and started walking on toward the house. "That's what I mean," she said. Then she stopped again. "Do you mind?" she said. "I think I'd rather go on by myself."

I said, "Of course. You go on. I'll go round a bit."

She nodded and walked on, and I stood there for a moment watching her go. Then I turned left-handed off the track and went in among the trees. We were near the edge of the wood here, and it was not so thickly grown. I could even get a glimpse of the house every now and then between the branches. I moved round in a circle, keeping my distance from it. The wind had gone, and the wood was very quiet. I was suddenly conscious of the silence, and went through it as quietly as I could.

After a bit the ground started to rise and I knew I was coming to the edge of the saucer. Then quite suddenly the trees stopped and there was nothing but the bare hillside in front of me. The house was back over my right shoulder now, with just the edge of the wood between me and it. I went straight on, scrambling up the face of the hill. It was surprisingly steep, and the rock came out everywhere through its thin covering of turf. I was not surprised that the trees stopped where they did. What soil there was had drained off into the bottom of the saucer, and the sheep, if there had been sheep, would have done the rest. I wondered what happened to the water that must come down off the surrounding hills. From what I had seen, no stream ran out through the gap in the hills where the road was. There might be standing water somewhere in the middle of the saucer. I seemed to remember that most abbeys had their fishponds. Even so, there must be an overflow somewhere. I thought that some time I would walk round the edge of the hills, just clear of the top of the trees, and try to get a better picture of the place.

For the moment all I wanted was to get back to the house without seeming to have come from the middle of the wood. When I was high enough up, I turned right-handed and made my way eastward along the face. I could see the chimneys of the house now over the tops of the trees. The hill came round in a sharp curve, and suddenly the trees dropped back and I was almost over the north gables. I was not too high to be seen, certainly not from the upstairs windows, and at once I turned and began scrambling down toward the house. So long as no one had seen me come out from round the edge of the wood, I was all right now. I had been up on to the hillside and now I was coming down. It was anyone's guess where I had gone up. But I hoped no one would ask.

In fact, no one did, because when I came into the hall, I heard Merrion and his sister talking in the sitting room. The door was shut. Their voices were so much alike, heard like that, that it took me a moment to tell which was which. It was only when one voice said, "But I asked him to stay a day or two more if he wanted to," that I knew it was Cynthia's. By then I had stopped and was quite deliberately listening.

Merrion said, "I don't see why he should want to. There is nothing for him to do here."

There was a moment's silence. Then Cynthia said, "I should have thought the important thing was not to let him think you want him to go. I've told you before how important that is."

There was no mistaking the authority. Merrion's voice, when it came, was almost sulky. "My dear girl," he said, "I know that. Only—"

Cynthia said, "He's not the sort of person to make trouble." I thought there was a slight emphasis on the "he." I turned and tiptoed back to the front door. I opened it quietly and shut it again with a bit of a bang. Then I walked firmly across to the sitting room door. I had just got there when I saw Ethel Merrion standing in the door of the kitchen. I did not know how long she had been there. I opened the door of the sitting room and went in.

CHAPTER 6

I HAVE NEVER SEEN a household in which four people lived so much their own lives, unsubjected to any sort of cohesive pressure. Each of the four of us seemed to have established a relation with each of the rest, of varying degrees of intensity; but all these separate relations remained separate, as if we touched each other on one side only. Wherever three or four of us were involved, the thing remained at an entirely superficial level. I was certain this was not my experience alone. It was the way the household worked before I ever came into it. It suited me, and in other circumstances I think I should have found it rather pleasant. As it was, it was disturbing, because I spent too much time wondering what all the other relations were. Also, I could not help wondering what Dick must have made of it, and what it would have made of Dick. All the same, it was my relation with Cynthia that mattered, and that was the one which, right through the whole business, never really changed in its essentials.

In the meantime, whatever the mental relations were, I was left physically very much to my own resources. I had been wrong in thinking someone might come after me if I was seen going into the wood. I was not one to make trouble. I had heard enough of what was said between Cynthia and her brother to know that this would be the accepted view. I walked out of the front door and round the north end of the house early in the afternoon. I do not know if anyone saw me go or not, or if they did, what they thought of it. I went in along the track. I had changed my mind about walking round the circle of the hills above the edge of the trees. I did not think I should see very much that way, except possibly whether there was a way out for the water which I thought must accumulate somewhere in the middle of the wood. Instead I had decided to walk round the perimeter wall of the abbey precinct, or what was left of it. I should be in the wood all the way, but I could not lose myself. All I had to do was follow the course of the wall for its full circle, and it would bring me back to the track again. In the meantime, I could see the abbey site, what there was to see of it, from all round. I walked until I felt the slight rise in the track under me and saw the green shoulders of the banks through the trees on both sides. I hesitated, turned right and went straight in toward the right-hand bank.

I was surprised at once by the size of it. The shoulder I had seen from the track was only the beginning of it. From there it rose steadily, until by the time I was well into the wood and out of sight of the track, I found myself on the flat top of a considerable earthwork. Below me, on my left hand as I walked, the ground fell away into a shallow ditch. The top of the bank was covered with moss and the coarse woodland grass, but the thick undergrowth was missing. Over the moss and grass the dead leaves were drifted everywhere. They were the leaves of God knows how many summers, lying one on top of the other in successive layers of decay. The trees grew close, so close that at times even the outline of the earthwork and its course ahead were doubtful. The trees could not obliterate these man-made defenses, but even from here they muffled and obscured them, and from the air, as Merrion had said, they would hide them completely. I picked my way between the trunks, keeping always to the causeway of higher ground. I made very little noise padding over the soft stuff. If I stopped, the silence was complete. I was glad I was on top of the bank. The trees were just as high and thick above me, but I did not feel quite so shut in.

All the same, I was puzzled by it, and the further I went, the more puzzled I became. I knew nothing whatever about the layout of Cistercian abbeys, or indeed of any other sort, but I found it very difficult to reconcile this great bank and ditch with the tumbled and half-buried stonework I had seen nearer the center of the wood. There were stones every now and then. There would be, in a place like this. They lay half in and half out of the leaves, and were themselves grown over with moss, but they were few and far between, and they did not look like dressed stones. For the rest, it seemed all earth, man-made at some time, and with immense labor, but not in any sense a piece of building, or even the remains of one. It might for all I knew be medieval, but it might be of any age. As far as I could, I kept an eye on the inner side of the ditch, but I saw no sign of anything that looked like building there either. That was not to say it was not there. The undergrowth grew thick again on the far side, and you could not see much.

Going like that, and always in a curve, I found it very difficult to tell how far I had gone or which way I was now facing. The sun might have been anywhere, and in that cluttered wilderness it was impossible to keep any sense of direction. But on time alone I thought I must by now be halfway round the circle and so facing south again. It was here, perhaps at the point furthest from the house, that I saw the first recognizable signs of relatively recent human activity. They were very slight, and I did not stop to investigate them, but for a short stretch on the inner side of the ditch the earth seemed to have been disturbed. The leaves still lay thick over everything, but between the leaves the earth and its green covering looked softer and not quite in order. As I say, I did not take any particular notice of it, but I should have said the whole stretch was fifteen or twenty yards long. I thought of it as a trial excavation, as if someone had been making a cautious investigation of the side of the ditch. I assumed it was Merrion, looking for traces of building inside his perimeter wall. Whoever it was, and whatever he had found, he had put everything back in order as far as he could in a proper and professional manner. I thought I might ask him about it some time. My mind was indeed full of questions, only I was not sure whether Merrion wanted me to ask them. Even on principle, I thought he was a man who disliked being asked anything. For the first time I wondered how far Cynthia shared his professional interests and was in his professional confidence. I thought she would be if anyone was. I was quite sure that Ethel Merrion was not. His confidences with her would be of another sort. I did not doubt, even now, that they existed. Cynthia had said they were very much man and wife. I did not know quite what that meant, and did not much like the sound of it, but I knew it meant something.

It was soon after this that I heard the sound of running water. It came from my right, and as I went on it got louder, until I knew there was a stream of sorts running through the wood and probably closing in at a tangent on the curve of the bank. I went on, expecting to see it at any moment. Then I realized that the sound was getting fainter. I went back until once more the water sounded quite close. Then I turned and went toward it. I went down the bank and pushed my way through the thicket at the bottom. There it was, at once. It was a sizable brook, running a straight course as far as I could see it, but to all appearances in a natural channel. It ran quite close to the outer side of the bank, passed it and disappeared again into the wood. I still did not know where the stream ran out of the saucer, but otherwise the thing was natural enough. What I did wonder was where the abbey got its water from. I knew that the monks' ideas of sanitation were in advance of their time, and they would want running water, fishponds or no fishponds. I supposed they could have piped it in, but that sounded altogether too modern. Some sort of an artificial feeder channel seemed more likely, something in the style of a millrace, which would take off the water they wanted for their domestic purposes and return it to the natural channel lower down. If that was what they had had, this would surely be one of the key points, where the natural channel came closest to their boundary. I did not know whether they had brought their water in here or let it out, but in either case there ought to be something to show.

There was no break in the top of the bank, because I had already walked uninterrupted past the point where the stream came closest. The only possibility, ruling out pipes, was some sort of culvert that would carry the water under the bank. I went back to the bottom of the bank, and at once I had what I wanted. The edges of two or three worked stones stood out at a stiff vertical from the sloping face of the bank. Below them, half buried in the earth, there was a tumble of stones, including at least two which looked like the voussoirs of a smallish roundheaded arch. It was impossible to tell which way the water was moving, or what its course had been once it was clear of the bank. But that it had gone under the bank was certain. The monks had driven a tunnel right through the bottom of the earthwork and to all appearances had roofed it with a masonry vault. It was the order of events which was significant. If the bank was simply the perimeter wall of the abbey, it was a very odd way of going about it. But unless I was very much mistaken, the bank had been there first.

I scrambled back to the top of the bank and went on with my walk. I saw no more signs that the bank had been pierced at any point, but without the stream to call attention to them I could have walked over the remains of half a dozen culverts and never noticed them. It was still completely quiet in the wood, and I did not hear the sound of water anywhere. Nor did I find any other obvious opening in the bank itself. It varied a good deal in height and shape. In places, perhaps where the soil was lighter, there had been a lot of silting, so that the whole contour was flatter and the ditch much less noticeable. But the main alignment was never in doubt. It ran on unbroken and always in the same steady curve, until suddenly, when my sense of direction and distance were fairly completely lost, it stopped altogether.

The green ridge fell away under my feet and the trees suddenly thinned in front of me. I went on down the slope, forced my way through a tangle of bushes at the bottom and came out on to a rutted green track running through the trees to right and left of me. For a moment I was filled with that curious feeling of vertigo you experience when your sense of direction is suddenly upset. I was still so conscious of having left the track behind me that I found it impossible to believe that this was the same track here in front. Then common sense reasserted itself over my outraged sense of direction. I had only done what I had all along intended to do. I had come full circle and was back where I had started. I still had very little idea what the total circumference was, but it must be very large indeed. Here, in the middle of this natural saucer in the hills and completely buried under the trees, the earthwork ran its great circle round some once calculated center. Inside it, and no doubt spread over the central point, the tumbled remains of the abbey lay in utter desolation. Here at my feet, coming straight in from the east like the solitary spoke of an enormous wheel, the track led into the hidden center from the single gap in the surrounding hills. And across the track Sir Josiah Braithwaite's stone house stood up squarely, blocking the way. I had thought, coming in the first evening under that fiery sky, that it was an extraordinary place, but I had not known the half of it.

Perhaps to reassure myself, I crossed the track and went up on to the opposite shoulder of the bank, where I had started my walk round. It was growing dusky in the wood already, and it was still completely quiet. I sat down on the sloping turf. I did not want to go back to the house just yet. I was more tired that I had expected, and I wanted to think. I could just see, over the tops of the bushes, the level green line of the track broken regularly by the vertical lines of the tree trunks. My eyes fixed themselves on the pattern of horizontal green and vertical gray, but they were only half in focus. I did not hear a sound, but the pattern was suddenly broken by movement on the left, and my eyes adjusted themselves, so that the whole thing came up sharply. Someone came along the track from the direction of the house. I could see only the top half of her, but I knew at once that it was Ethel Merrion. No one else moved like that. She went quickly across, appearing and disappearing behind the tree trunks. It was like the effect of an old cinematograph film, where the individual stills are clear enough, but do not quite marry up into continuous motion. Also, like an old film, it was completely silent. As she went, she turned her head over her shoulder and looked at something behind her.

Then, when she was halfway across the pattern, she disappeared. In fact, of course, she failed to reappear. She vanished behind one of the tree trunks and did not come out on the other side of it. Or not when I expected her to. Her appearance was probably delayed by only a second or two, but I found it extraordinarily disconcerting. When she did reappear, she had turned and was moving very slowly backward. Her head was back, too. Her hands hung limply at her sides, and she stared fixedly down the track toward the house. I still could not see the lower half of her, and the slow backward movement of this motionless torso had something very odd about it, as if she were floating backward on water. It carried her out of sight behind the next tree, and I waited breathlessly for her to reappear. Now that I come to think of it, the whole thing must really have been compressed into not very many seconds, but it seemed to go on very much longer. The next thing I knew, she was out again, once more facing the way she was moving, and moving much faster, almost as if she was starting to run. I had only a side view of her face the whole time, but it looked completely expressionless. The next moment Merrion caught up with her.

He also came into the pattern from the left, toward the house, moving fast with his head thrust forward and his arms a little outstretched. I do not think he was running, but he must have been walking very fast. As with her, what I could see of him moved all of a piece. There was still no sound anywhere. It was only as he came up with her that the upper parts of their bodies took life. His arms went out to grasp her, and she turned and her arms went up in front of her, for a moment as if she was trying to ward him off. Then they closed round his neck, and her head fell limply back as his face came down over hers. Neither of them said anything, even then.

I sat there, watching the frenzied dumb show compulsively, but not liking it at all. For a moment or two longer it went on, half hidden behind the trees as the locked bodies swayed backward and forward. Then they disappeared altogether below the tops of the bushes, and there was nothing to see or hear anywhere. I might have been alone in the wood. I drew my knees up, clasping my arms round them and sinking my head over my arms. If there was anything to see now, I did not want to see it. There was nothing to hear. I waited like that for quite a long time. When I lifted my head, it was almost completely dark, and I was very cold. I did not think there would be anyone on the track now. If there was, I need not see them nor they me. I got up stiffly and stumbled down through the bushes. I made no attempt to be quiet about it. I came out on to the track facing toward the house and set out at once on my walk back.

CHAPTER 7

THE WIND GOT UP with nightfall, and by the time I went to bed, which was early, it was blowing quite hard. My room faced south. The room next to it, which had been Dick's, faced west. They were both small rooms. Across the corridor there was a bathroom and another room, which must have been a spare room of some sort. I never saw anybody go into it. At the other end of the corridor, beyond the head of the stairs, the Merrions had a big room, with Cynthia's room and I think another bathroom opposite. Nobody used my end of the corridor at night except me, and once I was in my room I never heard anything from any other part of the house. As was to be expected of it, Sir Josiah's house was solidly built.

I switched the light on as I went into my room and shut the door behind me. I went toward the window and then, on an afterthought, went back to the door and switched the light off again. The corridor outside was brightly lit, but not a gleam came through the still superb Victorian joinery, and the floor was carpeted to the doorway. I groped my way back to the window and threw back the curtains. The cloud had broken before the wind, and there was a half moon riding high to the southward with a steady drift of small clouds blowing across it. The world was full of pale moving light, and through the half-open casement I could hear the wood roaring behind the house. Even in the moonlight you could see the first of the dead leaves flying. It was a disturbing sort of night, and I had had enough to disturb me as it was.

I pushed the casement fully open and leant out. It was not at all cold. The wind was westerly, and soft. There was enough of it to set the dry oaks roaring, but there was no bite in the air. It was the movement of the light and the noise of the leaves that counted. The light moved slower than the wind and the leaves on the trees faster, but between them they made you aware of it. You hardly felt the wind itself. I could not get the Merrions out of my mind, and their dreadful wordless love-making, as if they had only one channel of communication. Everybody had been very spruce and correct over dinner, but they had not said very much to each other, even then. Love-making seemed too polite a phrase in the circumstances, but in God's name, who was I to pontificate about love? All I knew was that I could not stop thinking about what I had seen, and that the more I thought about it, the more it disturbed me. Also, somewhere in the back of my mind I thought of the dancing man, all alive now in the moving moonlight, capering on his stone in solitary, ageless anticipation. The whole thing was intolerable. I pulled the window shut and flicked the curtains across it. I found my way back to the door in the sudden darkness and silence, but instead of switching the light on I opened the door quietly and put my head out. The corridor was as brightly lit as ever, but there was no sound anywhere. I went out and shut the door behind me, as quietly as I had opened it. Then I tiptoed along the corridor and down the stairs. The hall was lit, too, but the doors into the sitting room and dining room were open and both rooms in darkness. The front door had a single box-lock with the key turned in it. I turned the key back. Nothing made any noise in that house if you did not want it to. I opened the door, stepped out and shut it behind me. The noise of the wind in the wood closed round me at once. It took me a moment or two, after the brightly lit hall, to see how much light there was outside. Then I turned right and began to walk round the southern end of the house.

There were always only the two ways to walk, eastward along the tarmac to the village or westward along the green track into the wood. North and south the hillsides reared up, fit to scramble on by daylight, but not places for a solitary man to walk at night when he was too upset to sleep. So I went round the south side of the house and walked to the wood again. I do not think I admitted it to myself, but it was Cynthia I wanted to meet. I had never seen Cynthia in the wood. I did not know if she ever went there. I supposed she must sometimes. She was the only one of the four of us who had not been there already that day. Or as far as I knew. The house was putty-colored in the moonlight, with one warm pink patch high up in the western wall. There were lights on still in the Merrions' room, but the curtains were closely drawn, and inside the house there was not a murmur of voices anywhere, even from behind shut doors. I stood there for a moment or two in the noisy half-light, looking up at the window, as restless as a sex-struck adolescent. Then I turned and went into the wood.

I had lost my fear of it now. It held no answer for me, but the roaring of the wind in the trees and the washed-out intermittent light suited my mood. When I came to the gap in the earthwork, I stood there as I had stood under the curtained window, looking down at the smooth silver turf under the edge of the bushes, as if there must be something there to see. Then I walked on, slowly, with my hands behind my back and my head down. I did not really expect to meet anyone now. I came to the stone as unexpectedly as I had that first evening. I never seemed to know how far it was.

I stopped about fifteen yards from it, suddenly unwilling to go any further. I could see it quite clearly, standing straight up and motionless, while the trees threshed about over it. For the first time the air struck cold, and I wondered what the hell I was doing out there when I ought to be quiet and warm in my bed. I started to turn my back on it, and then the dancing man came out from behind it, white all over and capering in the moonlight, with his white matchstick arms straight up over his head. I had once held my school record for the hundred yards, but I had never run as I ran now. The wood roared all round me, and his kicked-up feet had made no sound at all as he danced on the turf. I could not have heard him if he had been prancing just behind me, but I was not going to turn my head or stop to look. I did not, even then, think it was the dancing man himself, magnified more than life-size, come down off the stone. I thought it was old Evans, but I still did not want him anywhere near me in that state.

I did not stop until I got my hand on the front-door handle. Then I dropped on my knees on the step, fighting to get my breath back and looking at the empty moonlit gravel in front of the house. I could feel the sweat running down my back, cold already under my clinging clothes. After a bit, when I could breathe without making too much noise about it, I opened the door, slipped inside and locked it behind me.

It was only then I noticed that the lights were all out. There was reflected moonlight in the hall from the windows on each side of the front door, but the lights which had blazed in the hall and along the corridor at the top of the stairs had all been turned out. Unless there was a time-switch, or some sort of master switch upstairs, that meant that someone had been around since I went out.

Whether they knew I had gone I had no way of telling. At least they had not locked me out, which in the circumstances I was glad of. I tiptoed over to the stairs. Cynthia was standing three or four stairs up, waiting for me. I knew at once who it was. This was the meeting I had been looking for ever since I left my room. In any case, she stood facing what light there was, and there was no mistaking the great wide-open eyes under the helmet of dark hair. She was swathed from neck to ankle in something dark. I stopped when I saw her, and then went slowly up the stairs to her. She did not move at all. My breathing was still a bit noisy and I was inclined to shiver.

She said, "Have you been in the wood?" We spoke in whispers. I did not know whether the Merrions were still awake. I had not given as much attention to their window on my way home as I had going out.

I said, "Yes." I went up to the stair just below her and stood there. She put her hands out and took hold of my arms just above the elbow, looking at me intently in the faint light.

"Something frightened you?" she said.

I started to nod, but the nod turned to a shiver that shook me all over. "Yes," I said again.

Her hands tightened a little on my arms. "You mustn't go," she said. "Not at night. I don't think it's safe."

I said, "Not after all these centuries?"

She looked at me for a moment and then shook her head. "Still not," she said.

I nodded again. This time I managed to move only my head. "Promise you won't," she said. "Not at night."

I thought I could feel the warmth of her body on my face. I wondered if she had come out of her bed. I needed warmth above everything. I said, "Don't you ever go there?"

"Sometimes. Not at night."

"I wanted to see you," I said. I think I must have started to move toward her, because I was suddenly conscious of her arms between us, gentle but quite unyielding, keeping me at my distance.

She said again, "Not at night. Not in the wood."

I thought for a moment, not very coherently, but could not think of anything else to say. She said, "Go on up now. Have a hot bath and get to bed. There's nothing to be frightened of here."

There was nothing in the least patronizing or derisive in this. She was simply stating a fact. I found it very comforting. She let go of my arms suddenly and stood aside. "Go on," she said.

I went up past her. I had not touched her at all all this time. Now as I went past her I put out a hand and just touched her. Her wrap was soft, and she was warm under it, as I knew she would be. "Thank you," I said. "Good night, Cynthia." She did not answer, and I went on upstairs, leaving her standing there.

I slept deeply, but awoke a little the worse for wear, both in body and mind. I still felt twinges of almost incredulous horror at the thing I had run away from in the wood. My mind was busy rationalizing the thing itself, but I could not forget my own terror. More mundanely, I was stiff and uneasy from my run, and had a sore throat, despite the hot bath I had obediently soaked myself in before I went to bed. When I got out of bed, I found I had pulled a muscle in the back of one heel, and was going a little lame. The slight ridiculousness of this only served to drive home the fact that I had bolted in stark panic for the first time in my life. It is not a common experience nowadays, in peacetime and in a civilized country. It was going to take a bit of getting over. My eyes met Cynthia's once over the breakfast table, and she looked long and gravely at me. Merrion was as urbane and hesitant as ever. Ethel Merrion was as elusive as a bird, but I was suddenly and guiltily aware that her physical attraction had taken on a sharper edge, so that I could hardly keep my eyes off her. The guilt I felt had no reference to Merrion. The whole situation was becoming unbearably complicated, and I thought it was time I was gone.

After breakfast I followed Merrion into the hall and said, "I think I should be moving on tomorrow."

"Yes?" he said. "Well—if you must, of course. You'll take your brother's things?"

I had the clearest possible feeling that what he really wanted to know was that he was getting rid, once and for all, of the whole Hawkins family. "I will," I said.

He said, "Good," and the sense of relief was unmistakable under the tone of mild approval.

"In any case," I said, "you'll be getting back to Bristol yourself soon, I imagine."

"That's right, yes, only another week." He nodded and went off to his room and I went upstairs. I went toward my room and then turned into the room next to it, where Dick's suitcases were. I shut the door behind me and pulled one of the cases out from under the bed. I knew which one I wanted. I thought I knew now what it was that Ethel Merrion had had in her hand when I had found her in here that first evening. I pulled out the clothes I had left folded on top and slipped a hand in, feeling for the medallion on its leather lace. I even thought I knew whereabout in the case I had put it, but I could not find it there. I put the clothes from the top on one side and took everything else, piecemeal, out of the case. The medallion was not there. I repacked the case. I did not think I could have been mistaken, but to make sure I pulled the other case out from under the bed and searched that. The medallion was not there, of course.

It never for a moment occurred to me that there was any great mystery here. Anyone could have come in and taken the thing at any time, but I had no doubt at all who had. I was conscious only of a slight disappointment, and that not a very respectable one. I had had it in mind to give Ethel the medallion myself, and I was upset that she had forestalled me. What I had hoped to get out of the gesture I did not stop to examine. I shut the two cases and left them standing just inside the door of the room, ready for me to take down to my car next day. Then I went downstairs and out of the house to have a look at the car itself.

I had not touched it since the morning after my arrival, when at Merrion's suggestion I had driven it into one of the outbuildings and shut the door on it. I had had a long drive here, and thought I had better do the usual checks before I took it back on the road. In fact there was not much that needed doing. I needed petrol, but could get that in the village on my way out. I started to make my way out between the side of the car and the wooden wall of the shed. The shed was only just big enough to take the car, and it was a bit of a squeeze. As I moved, my arm caught a sacking curtain tacked on to the studs of the wall, and the bottom corner of it tore away from the tacks. There was a gleam of glass behind it, but not much light on the far side. The shed was a lean-to built on to the side of a larger building, which I had noticed was padlocked on the outside. The padlock had not struck me as anything unusual. In a place like this most people would keep their outbuildings locked, especially when Cynthia was alone in the house much of the time and there were people as odd as old Evans about. But a casually uncovered window giving on to a locked building will kindle a mild curiosity in most people. I lifted the flap of sacking and peered through the glass.

What immediately struck me was that the other side of the glass had also been covered, with what looked like thick paper, but on that side too the covering had been slightly torn. My flap of sacking overlapped the tear in the paper just enough to afford a peephole into the locked building. With a purely idle curiosity and no sense at all of shame, I rubbed my side of the dusty glass with a finger and peered through the gap. There must have been a skylight of some sort in the roof, because although the door was shut, there was a certain amount of rather murky daylight in the place. Even by moving my head from side to side I could see only a very limited area. It was full of stacked stuff which suggested surveying equipment of some sort. This was probably because of a bundle of marked poles leaning against the opposite wall. The rest was pretty miscellaneous. There was what looked like a measuring chain, a box of pegs and I thought digging tools. I could only see the ends of the handles, but they suggested spades or shovels and probably picks or fencing mauls. I remembered the signs of digging on the inner side of the earthwork. I wondered whether, with all this gear, Merrion had not in fact done more digging on the site than he seemed ready to admit, and if so, why he should be so cagey about it. I supposed there was an element of professional jealousy in it. He had made no bones about his pleasure in having the site to himself. All the same, I did not see why his caginess should extend to an uninstructed outsider like me.

I started to move away from the window. The movement gave me an unexpected and momentary glimpse of a new section of floor. What I saw there seemed so unlikely that I was moving back for a second look when I heard someone coming across the gravel outside the shed. I pulled the sacking back over its tacks and scrambled toward the door. When I got there, Merrion was still seven or eight yards away and well to one side. He could not possibly have seen what I was doing. I smiled at him and began to shut the doors of the shed. He came up with his head a bit down, looking at me from under heavy eyebrows as he had the first time I had seen him. He said, "Everything all right?"

"Yes," I said, "she's all ready for the road. There's not much petrol, but I'll get some in the village." I shut the door of the shed firmly and turned to meet him as he came across the gravel. I stood there facing him. I thought he would have walked past me to the shed if he had been able to think of a single reason for doing so, but nothing occurred to him. We just stood there, looking at each other. It was exactly as it had been outside the door of Dick's room on the night of my arrival, and I knew exactly what he was going to say next.

"Well—" he said. After a bit he gave it up. He turned, and we walked back toward the house together. We made some sort of incoherent conversation. I do not know what was in his mind while he was talking. I know what was in mine. I was wondering why in the world he needed wire ropes and, unless I was mistaken, a fairly formidable assortment of blocks and tackle. I wondered if he had been uprooting trees. I could think of no other explanation.

CHAPTER 8

I DID NOT SEE Cynthia alone during the rest of the day. With the household working the way it did, this did not necessarily mean that she was avoiding me, but I thought she might be. There were too many questions left unanswered between us. I do not think in fact I should have asked them, but she could not know that. I packed my own things during the afternoon, as far as I could. I was anxious to be away now. I did not want to go without talking to Cynthia, but I was still anxious to go. I had not made anything very clear to myself, but I did not, even at that stage, believe that I should never see her again.

The wind had gone and the cloud had come back over the sky. It was going to get dark early. There was not a sound from the wood now. It was still very mild. I went out after tea to walk to the stone and back. I wanted to do it before it got dark, but I wanted to do it. I had reasoned the business out with myself, but there were still things left in my mind which I did not want left there. I went back to outface them if I could, rather as a man who has fallen off a horse is supposed to get back in the saddle again as soon as possible, before his fright has had time to settle.

There was another thing in my mind, too. I had told

Cynthia I had hoped to see her in the wood and asked her if she never went there. She had said she did, sometimes. I thought that if I went into the wood on this last evening before I left, she might, if she chose, manage to meet me there. I did not know if she would choose, but I wanted to give her the choice. I thought if I could only meet Cynthia at the stone, the thing would never haunt me again. Even without her I could still outface it, but with her I could lay it for ever. I walked on steadily in the dusky silence. By this time tomorrow I should be a couple of hundred miles away. It occurred to me to wonder whether I should then accept as real the present painful confusion of my feelings, but as I got further along the track, everything merged in a huge, undefined apprehension. The only thing that drove me now was the simple determination to get there and back.

By the time I went through the gap in the earthwork it was already darker than I had expected. If anyone had been standing in the trees by the side of the track now, I do not think I should have seen them. I had meant to have another steady look at the dancing man, but it was not going to be possible. I had no sort of light with me. The odd thing was that this time, when I was full of apprehension, the stone did not take me by surprise. I knew quite well that I was coming to it, and there it was. I walked straight up to it, touched it and walked round it. The person who was waiting on the other side of it walked straight into my arms. I cannot pretend that I had even a moment's doubt who it was. It was Ethel Merrion.

Everything went up in an instantaneous, breathless upsurge of pent-up desire. We neither of us said anything. The face she turned up to meet mine was white in the darkness and her eyes were shut. Our bodies simply took charge. It was a quick, violent love-making, with a touch of desperation in it. It was also extraordinarily sweet. She was a sweet person. In some remote, detached corner of my mind I still knew it was Cynthia I had come out to see, and I never for a moment doubted that behind Ethel Merrion's shut eyes I was standing in for Dick. This did not seem to matter in the least. I can only hope the dancing man approved of what was going on at his feet. I think he should have. I am not at all sure that he was not at least partly responsible for it.

Even when it was all over, no one made any attempt to explain anything. The first time I spoke to her was when we were already halfway back to the house. I said, "You have got Dick's medal, haven't you?"

She said, "Yes. I took it. You don't mind, do you?"

"No," I said, "I was going to give it to you anyhow."

She made no comment on this. I remembered, with a sort of mild, sardonic amusement, that I had wanted to gain her favor, in some undefined way, by giving her the medallion. Now, when we had neither of us anything further to give, my intended gesture seemed after all to make very little impression. Instead she said, "Did you know about it? I mean, before you found it among his things."

"I knew about it, but I had forgotten. I remember his being given it when he was a boy."

She nodded. "I know. He told me."

I said, "I suppose he wore it for luck."

She said, "Yes. Yes, that's it." I knew then when and how she had seen the medallion. I remembered Dick's little bit of cheerful, characteristic bravado about difficult ascents. I could not tell her this, but I reckoned he had worn it for more than one kind of luck. I turned and found her looking up at me as we walked. Even in the darkness I could see that her face had hardened again, and when she spoke, there was a touch of impatience in it. "That's it," she said. "Don't you see?"

I stopped. She stopped too, and we faced each other.

Suddenly and sickeningly, I thought I did see. "Don't you see?" she said again. "It shouldn't be there. Not if he was climbing."

I said, "But—" and stopped. I was trying to get the thing in some sort of focus in my mind. After a bit I said, "His climbing gear was gone."

She nodded, quite calmly and quite relentlessly. "Oh yes," she said. "They thought of that, of course. But they didn't know about this. So it got left."

I said again, "But—" but she did not let me go on. She said, "Do you know what else is missing?"

"No," I said, "of course I don't. I don't know what he had."

"That's it. That's it, you see. He might have been anywhere, doing anything, wearing anything, when he died. We don't know. All I do know is that he wasn't climbing. And they say he was."

I said, "Where were you, then?"

"That day? I was away. That one day I was away. I went to the dentist. Of all damned things, I went to the dentist. And when I came back, quite late in the evening, they said he was missing. Of course I didn't think—I thought he'd come back. I went on thinking that, right through it all. I even thought—well, you remember, that first evening you came. Then later, that same evening, I found the medal. Then I knew. But I don't know anything else—just that he wasn't climbing." She turned and started to walk on again. We were very close to the house now. Just before we got there, she said, "You are going tomorrow, aren't you?"

I said, "Yes, I'm going." I thought she was going to ask another question, which I did not know how to answer. Or not yet. I had to have time. But she did not ask it. We neither of us said anything more at all. The first time I had met her in the wood, I had held her for a moment or two in my arms, on false pretenses, admittedly, but I had held her, and we had walked in together as if nothing had happened. The second time we had had a few minutes' conversation, but we had parted and gone home deviously and come in by different ways. This time we had made love and talked of murder, and we walked in together as if nothing had happened. It was all very strange. But no one was about and no one saw us come in, so I suppose it did not matter.

I went straight up to my room. The first thing I did was to get rid of the various evidences of what I had been doing, for all the world like a guilty husband come back from an escapade and anxious to straighten himself up before his wife gets near him. As usual, it was not Merrion I was thinking of. Then I sat on the edge of my bed and tried to straighten myself up mentally as I already had physically. Here again, it was not Merrion that was the trouble. I think I should have been ready to believe anything of him, not so much because I disliked and mistrusted him as because there was always, in any case, so much about him you did not know. It was Cynthia that my mind turned and turned on. Ethel Merrion had said "they," lumping brother and sister together as a matter of course. But she did not know. I kept on telling myself that. She could not know any more than I could. If something had happened to Dick which was not an accident, Cynthia might have accepted her brother's account of it, just as Ethel herself had to start with. On the other hand, Cynthia had been here that day, and Ethel had not. And over and above that, I did not really believe that Merrion could keep his sister in the dark for long if he had got involved in anything as serious as that. I did not even believe he would want to. His dependence on her was too great. I did not know at all what had happened to Dick. Like Ethel Merrion, I only knew what had not happened to him. That I knew, as she did, on the strength of the medallion, because we both knew Dick. I had forgotten the thing's existence all these years, but once I had seen it again, I knew, as surely as she did, that he would not have gone climbing without it. So he had not been killed climbing, but someone, after his death, had taken his climbing gear out of his room and got rid of it. Whatever had happened to start with, that had been deliberate and calculated. And by that stage, at least, I found it almost impossible to believe that Merrion had been on his own.

I got up, looked myself over once more in the glass, and went out into the corridor. One thing at least was settled. Whatever had happened, I had to know. I could not leave things as they were. I turned and walked along the corridor. Cynthia was coming along it from the opposite direction. Her eyes held mine all the way along, and when we met at the top of the stairs, it seemed as if we should never be able to turn aside and go down them. The startling thing was that what had happened between me and Ethel Merrion and what I had in my mind about Dick did not seem to affect in any way the feeling I had for her. At least, I found it startling at the time, but I am not sure, in fact, that I should have. My experience is that moral judgments of any sort are extraordinarily slow to alter the way you feel about a person. I suppose if a man you like very much suddenly stabs you in the back, you may be forced, however unwillingly, to revise your opinion of him, but if you merely see him stab someone else, you will probably think he is still a nice man acting oddly for reasons unknown to you. It is his niceness that you are indefeasibly conscious of, and to this the moral quality of his actions seems irrelevant. It works the other way, too. I once caught a most dislikable man red-handed doing good by stealth, and it took me another year at least to learn to like him. If the other person is a woman you are by way of being in love with, the process of change will be even slower and more laborious. I still wanted to know the truth about Dick, but at the moment, there, at the head of the stairs, the one important thing was whether Cynthia would walk into my arms or whether she would at last turn and go down the stairs. She turned, and I turned, but only just. We went down together, not even touching. She said, "Ethel's not feeling well. She's gone to bed early. So there's only the three of us."

"I'm sorry," I said. I was not, of course, sorry in the least. I was pleased and relieved almost beyond expression. Also I was grateful to Ethel. I did not for a moment suppose that there was anything wrong with her, and I was extraordinarily glad of her absence. Merrion was waiting for us in the sitting room. I greeted him almost jovially. I was certainly not going to be bothered to feel guilty about him. I had done him no harm. I had reason, now, to suspect that if he knew what had happened, his reaction would be a tremendous explosion of grief and anger. But he did not, and I did not think he ever would. There was nothing to feel bad about. Cynthia went off to see about the meal, and I was left alone with him.

"I've been wondering," I said. "Where did the abbey get its water from? They must have had a supply."

"Oh yes," he said. "That was one of the things they made a great deal of. There's a stream, in fact. It collects from the northern slopes and runs fairly near the site."

"Runs where? I mean—where does it run out of the valley? Not on this side, that I've seen."

He was watching me all the time now, but it was all plain sailing so far. He said, "Not on this side, no. The whole valley floor in fact slopes very slightly from north to south. There is a narrow gap in the hills on the south side. The stream finds its way out there."

I nodded. I was all intelligent interest. "What did they do, then? Pipe it in?"

He allowed himself a quick half-smile. "Well," he said, "not pipe it in, exactly. That would have been a bit beyond them. No, I think they probably brought in an artificial channel through the site and fed it back into the main stream again further down."

"As for a water mill?"

"That's it. That's it, exactly. It was a familiar technique, after all. There may have been hatches of some sort to control the flow. I haven't gone into that yet."

"What about the bank?" I said.

He looked at me for what seemed quite a time. Then he said, "The bank?"

"The boundary wall," I said. "You said it surrounds the site."

"Ah. Yes. I fancy they brought the water under it."

I said, "The bank was there first?"

He turned away from me and went and took a book out from a shelf on the far side of the room. He opened the book and looked at it, but it was pure play-acting. "I told you," he said, "I have made no real examination of the site at all. I have certainly not tried to establish any sort of time sequence for the various works."

He was still looking at the book, and I spoke to his back. "I asked," I said, "because I was having a look at the bank yesterday. It's a very considerable earthwork, and I couldn't see any signs of masonry. I wondered whether it couldn't be a good deal older than the monastic building. I mean—I don't know much about these things, but it looked to me more like what one sees on a prehistoric site."

He shut the book and put it back in the shelf. He said, "When were you having a look at it?"

"Oh," I said, "yesterday, after lunch."

He nodded and came back toward me. He said, "I suppose it's possible. But without excavation—"

I said, "What did Dick think?"

"Dick?" he said. He said it as he had said it once before, almost as if he did not know who I was talking about.

"Dick," I said. "My brother. He was a prehistorian, after all. If there were any prehistoric features—"

Merrion's eyes were very wide open. They stared at me out of a face that looked darker than ever, as if it was flushed under the sallow skin. When he really looked at you straight, he could be very frightening. He said, "I did not discuss it with him at all."

Cynthia, in the doorway, said, "Shall we eat?" I did not know how long she had been there. Merrion and I disentangled our eyes and both turned and looked at her.

He said, "Yes. Good," and we all went through into the dining room. It was not a very cheerful meal, but we got through it well enough. I talked to both Merrion and his sister, and I thought very hard about them both, but what I was thinking had no connection at all with what I was saying. I knew Merrion had been on the defensive, and I knew he had been lying. I know very little about prehistoric sites, but I reckon I know when a man is lying and furiously angry that he has been made to lie. I had to go on now. It was not really because of Dick, or not wholly or directly. It was mainly because of Cynthia. I did not want to make trouble for her, but I could not leave her, as she now was, an apparent accomplice in something that might be pretty horrifying. Also, there was Ethel Merrion. I did not want to make trouble for her either, but she had deliberately planted in my mind her own suspicions. I did not know what she expected me to do about them, but I found it difficult to believe that she expected me to do nothing.

As for Cynthia herself, the one thing that really occupied my mind was whether I could see her again, privately, before I left. I always came to the same conclusion. If she wanted me to, I should. If not, there was very little I could do. I could not see myself tiptoeing along the corridor and tapping on her door during the night. Bedroom farce would not be in her line. In any case, her door was immediately opposite the Merrions'. I looked at her across the table, and kept the conversational ball rolling, and wondered what she would do.

She disappeared into the kitchen with the coffee tray, and almost at once Merrion excused himself on the ground of Ethel's being unwell. Whatever Ethel's symptoms were, he might in fact be worried about her, one way or another. But I think mainly he did not want to find himself alone with me. He said good night and I heard him go upstairs. I stayed on in the sitting room. I was not going up so long as Cynthia was in the kitchen. Once I was in my room, the thing was finished. I could not see her tapping on my door either.

I never heard her come out of the kitchen. I suddenly looked up and found her standing in the doorway, as I had earlier in the evening. She was looking at me. I do not know how long she had been looking at me, but I could read nothing in her face, nothing at all. When I looked up, she said, "I'm going up now."

I got up. "Then I will, too," I said.

We went up the stairs, with her ahead of me, just as we had the evening I had arrived. At the top she stopped and turned. For a second we looked at each other, a little desperately. Then she came to me and we kissed. It was not a very successful kiss, and it occurred to me, with an almost unbearable mixture of tenderness and exhilaration, that she did not know much about kissing. But I thought time would change that. Then we went off, each to our own end of the corridor. We did not say anything at all.

CHAPTER 9

The man smiled pleasantly at me as I came in, but his face had that watchful, oversensitized look I remembered seeing on Merrion's when I had first met him. That seemed a long time ago now, but of course the position was the same. I had come to see him about my presumably dead brother, and he was anxious not to start off-key. He said, "Mr. Hawkins? You're Dick's brother, of course. It was a sad business, that. They still haven't found him?"

"No," I said. "No, I don't think they will now. It must be difficult for you. What are you doing about his job?"

Some of the caution went out of his face. He smiled at me again, still cautiously, but gratefully. He said, "I'm glad you asked that. It was a point I wanted to raise with you. It is difficult, as you say. Legal presumptions apart, have you yourself any doubt that he is dead?"

For some reason, the figure of old Evans came into my mind, not the dancing man of my nightmare, but the scarecrow standing nine feet high in the gap in the hills chanting, "Dead he is, dead, and will never be found." I shook my head firmly at Dick's head of department. "No," I said, "none. I think you would be justified in proceeding on that assumption. What in fact are you doing?"

"Technically, we are treating it as a case of sabbatical leave. We have made temporary arrangements for his work. But if you think—" He looked at me inquiringly.

"I think you should go ahead with a permanent appointment," I said. "Mind you, I've no legal position in the matter. But for what it's worth, that is my view."

He said, "Thank you. That is very helpful. Now—is there something I can do for you?"

"There is," I said. "I'm afraid you may think it a little odd in the circumstances. If so, will you please overlook the apparent oddity? There is something I want to ask you. My reasons are purely personal—private, if you like—but if you can tell me, I shall be very grateful."

"Ask away," he said. "I'll answer if I can. And so far as I am concerned, it won't go any further."

I nodded. I said, "When Dick went up to this place—Llanglas, it's called—did he tell you he was going? And if so, did you gather it was purely a pleasure trip, for the climbing and so on, or was there any suggestion of a professional interest involved?"

He set his lips at that, but there was the beginning of a smile on them. "I see," he said. "At least, I don't see, quite, but I won't question your interest. Yes, he told me he was going. There was no question of an official report, you understand? It was in vacation. He didn't have to account for his time. He just mentioned it in conversation." He paused, looking at me. He was certainly smiling now. "You know the way Dick talked," he said. "At least—you're his brother—you must have known him even better than I did."

"I know how he talked, of course. What did he say, in fact?"

"I can't tell you exactly what he said. But the general effect was that it was business mixed with pleasure. Or so at least I understood. Things he was interested in. New finds he wanted to explore. You know the way he talked. One never quite knew how far to take him seriously."

I said, "The climbing and so on."

"Exactly. The climbing and so on." He paused again. "I knew who Merrion was—this man he was going to stay with—but I didn't know what his household consisted of, or who else might be there. It wasn't my job to inquire. But I assumed there was a—a center of interest somewhere. You know what Dick was like."

"Of course," I said. "I understand all that. But he did mention business? I mean—you got the impression that he really had some professional interest there, whatever others he may have had?"

He was looking at me a bit more seriously now. He took his time about it. Then he nodded. "Yes," he said. "I can't tell you exactly what gave me the impression, but I certainly had the impression that he was on to something. I didn't press him. There was no need, with Dick. If he'd found something, I should have heard all about it presently. There was no professional dog-in-the-mangerism with him, you know. Too little, really. Too little for his own good, I mean. It's a cut-throat trade, you know, being an academic these days."

"I see," I said. I thought for a moment, and he went on looking at me. Then I said, "Dick's speciality was the neolithic, wasn't it? Anything medieval—even Dark Ages stuff—would be out of his line?"

"Oh yes, completely. His best work to date was on the henge monument at Tredinas. He more or less discovered that. I mean—we knew there was something there from the aerial photographs, but he did the definitive excavation. It was very impressive."

"A henge monument," I said. "Stonehenge—that kind of thing? There's a Woodhenge, too, isn't there?"

"I'm sorry," he said. "It's a term we use. Yes, it's a type of construction peculiar to the British Isles. They don't exist anywhere else. We distinguish two main types, but essentially it's a circular bank-and-ditch construction with as far as we can tell a purely religious or cultural significance. I mean—not an occupation site.

and no question of defense or stock-herding or anything like that. A temple of some sort, not a fort or a stockade."

"A temple to what?" I said, but he shook his head.

"We don't know," he said. "I don't see how we ever can. We can make guesses. But it was something enormously powerful and important. The work that went into them was colossal and they lasted a long time. Avebury was a great religious center for at least a thousand years."

"I see. And that was Dick's main professional interest?"

"I should say so, certainly."

"He wouldn't—I mean, supposing there were signs of a thing like that existing that hadn't been recorded—a new site, do you see? Dick wouldn't be likely to have missed it?"

He did not try to disguise his interest, but he did no more than answer my question. "Not likely at all," he said. "On the contrary, I think he'd have been on to it like a terrier on a rathole." He looked at his hands for a moment. Then he looked at me again. He said, "We were talking of your brother just now—I don't know, a little lightly, perhaps. But he wasn't a lightweight professionally, you know. He was very keen on his job and very good at it."

"Thank you," I said. "That is just what I wanted to know."

He smiled at me rather ruefully. "You more or less put me under a vow of secrecy," he said. "I wish you hadn't. You can't tell me any more?"

I got up. "Not yet. But I think quite soon. In the meantime—I can rely on you? It is really very important."

He was standing now too. "I tell you what," he said. "I'll give you six months. I can't accept the permanent suppression of material, whatever your reasons. If you haven't come back to me by then, I'll start to follow up what you've suggested as best I can. And as Dick would have wished, if that's of any interest to you."

"It is," I said. "But six months will be more than enough. I'm enormously grateful to you." He waved a hand as if he had nothing more to say, and I bowed myself out. Six months, I thought. I had not much more than a fortnight's leave left, and there were at least three visits I had meant to pay. But the double compulsion was too strong. Nothing else really counted. Merrion and presumably Ethel would be back at Bristol by now. It was time I was back at Llanglas.

I did not intend to tell Cynthia I was coming. I thought that whatever she felt about it, my coming back would not surprise her. The one idea I had was that it would be better to arrive there after dark, and get through the village unseen, but in any case unrecognized. If I was going to be there any time, I had no doubt my presence would be known soon enough. Only if for any reason I did not stay, I did not see why anyone should know I had been there at all.

It was after nine when I drove in through the gap in the hills. It was pitch-dark, and I had not seen anyone since I left the main road on the other side of the village. When I got to the last bend in the road, I cut my lights and pulled in to the side. I waited until my eyes got used to the darkness. Then I started the car up again and crawled on, peering ahead until the lights of the house suddenly showed up in front. I went a bit faster then, with the lights reflected on the tarmac in front of me to show me the road. All the same, it was still pretty slow, and I made very little noise. I drove in through the gate, cut the engine and drifted to a halt on the gravel. The faint crunching of the wheels died away, and there was complete silence and complete darkness except for the lights of the house.

I got out. I left my cases where they were. I went as

quietly as I could across the gravel and up the front steps. I was still thinking that I might have some reason to go away again without even speaking to Cynthia. I did not know what that reason might be, unless the Merrions were back. At any rate, I wanted to see her before she saw me. I looked into the hall through one of the windows at the side of the door. I did not think it was as brilliantly lit as I remembered it, but this might be my imagination. There was no one there, and there were no lights on in the sitting room or dining room. The door of Merrion's working room was shut. I went down the steps and round the north end of the house toward the kitchen window. There were lights there. There were also lights on the floor above, which on this corner of the house meant Cynthia's bedroom. I went out a little wide from the end of the house and then turned and came in toward it. The upper window was curtained, and as I came in, the light behind it went out. I thought she would be coming downstairs. I was quite close to the kitchen window by now. I wondered whether to go back and watch her come down into the hall, but there was no time. The door on the opposite side of the kitchen opened and more lights were switched on. Cynthia came into the white brilliance, not ten yards from me, wearing a white overall.

Her dark hair was gathered on the nape of her neck. Against the unnatural whiteness all round it her skin looked the color of ivory. She seemed to have no make-up on at all. The whole picture should have been a bit austere, but she moved briskly, with a very slight smile on her face. I saw at once how right I had been to think she would never be lonely here. She looked so settled and content that I began to wonder whether after all she would really be glad to have me break in on her solitude. I thought there was only one relation in which she did not show a fairly complete self-possession. To me it was the most important relation of all, but it was not one I could expect to step straight into. And I still had to find out what she knew about Dick. Whatever it was, I did not think it would make me feel very differently about her. But that did not mean that she would be ready to tell me, even if she believed this. I watched her there in the kitchen, moving about white-overalled in a white world and knowing exactly what she was doing. I wanted too many incompatible things from her, and I did not really know how to set about getting any of them without losing the rest. All the same, I had to try.

There did not seem to be anyone else about. There could be no question of going now. I went back to the front of the house and walked across the gravel to my car. I thought even if she came out into the hall now, she could not know how long it had been there. I started the engine, watching the windows along the front of the house for any light or sign of movement. Nothing happened. I put the car in gear, switched on the lights and rolled her over those few yards of gravel to the front door. Then I stopped, switched off and turned off the lights, just as if I had that moment driven in from the road. Still nothing happened in the house. I got out, took my cases out and went up the front steps to the door. I had never noticed if there was a bell of any sort. I had assumed there must be, but now when I wanted it, I could not find one. I was still fumbling at the side of the door, when more lights went up in the hall and through one of the windows I could see a shadow moving. I knocked on the door. I was afraid it would startle her, and tried to make it sound as unalarming as possible. I do not know quite how I set about this, but in any case I do not think I need have worried. The door was locked, certainly, but she unlocked it and swung it open with no apparent hesitation.

In one thing, at least, I had been right. She was not surprised to see me. What else she was I could not tell.

I thought perhaps amused, for one thing. She looked at me a moment, smiling slightly. Then she stood back. "Hullo," she said. "Come in."

I stepped into the hall and put my cases down. "Do you mind?" I said.

I had shut the door behind me, and now she went past me and turned the key again in the lock. Then she turned and faced me. She shook her head. She said, "I thought you'd come."

"The same room?" I said.

"Yes, please. I'm afraid the bed's not made up. I wasn't as sure as all that. But it won't take any time." She thought for a moment. "Have you had a meal?"

"Oh yes."

"Where? I mean—not in the village?"

"No, no. Thirty miles back. I came straight through the village."

She nodded. "Good," she said. "Look—you take your cases up, and I'll get out sheets and things."

I started up the stairs with the cases. This time she came up behind me. When I got to the top, I put the cases down and turned. "You're not expecting your brother?" I said.

She had hesitated a few stairs down when I stopped, but now she came on up again. I had not left her very much room, but she got between my case and the corner of her side of the corridor, and stood there, in her own territory. I do not think either of us intended any symbolism in this, but once it had happened, we both recognized it. We faced each other across the invisible frontier at the head of the stairs. She had never crossed the line to my side while I had been there, and I had never crossed it to hers at all. We had always met and parted at the line. The last time we had parted, we had kissed. Before, she had shared her territory with the Merrions. Now she had it to herself. I knew, immediately and conclusively, that I must not cross the line uninvited. She looked at me for a moment or two. I think she was making sure I understood this. When she was sure, she answered my question. "No," she said. "They're not likely to come just yet. You don't want to meet him?"

I said, "I'm easier without him. You know that. It would be the same wherever I was. But of course—if he did come now and find me here, I should feel that my presence needed a bit of explaining."

"As it is, it doesn't?"

"You expected me," I said. "You must have had your reasons."

She nodded. "That's perfectly true. I don't know how far they're right."

"No more you would with my explanations," I said. "It's the same thing."

For the first time she looked a little unhappy. She hesitated. "I suppose not," she said. Then her face changed. She said, "Go on, you take your bags along. I'll get the other things." She turned and went off toward her end of the corridor. I picked up the cases and went along to my room. I put the cases down inside. Then I switched on the light and drew the curtains. When I came out again, she was coming along from her end with the linen in her hands. I think she wanted to see what I should do.

I went forward and met her at the head of the stairs. "Give that to me," I said. "I'll do the bed."

Her eyes were very wide open. Just for a moment the defenses were down. She looked vulnerable and very lovely. "Really?" she said.

"Really."

"Thank you," she said. She put the sheets and things into my hands, and I turned and went back to my room.

CHAPTER 10

When I had made up the bed and unpacked my things, I went downstairs and met Cynthia in the hall. "What about the car?" I said.

She said, "Oh yes, I'm glad you thought of that. I think you'd better put it away."

"I'll do it now," I said.

When I was at the door, she said, "Half a minute. The shed's locked. You'll need the key." She turned and went into the kitchen. I unlocked the front door and stood there waiting. She came back with a key in her hand. It was one of a bunch on a ring, but she held it apart from the rest. "Better lock up after you," she said.

I took the key, holding it, as she had, separate from the rest of the bunch. "I'll do that," I said. Just for a moment she looked at the keys in my hand. Then she nodded. I went out, shutting the front door behind me.

I got into the car and put the keys on the seat beside me. There were half a dozen of them, nothing very big or special. They looked like padlock keys. There seemed to be only one of each. I put them down carefully, so that the one I wanted did not get mixed up with the rest. Then I started the car, turned it on the gravel and drove round to the shed. I used only the side lights. There was a fairly ordinary padlock on the door of the shed. I opened it, leaving the key in the lock, and swung the doors back. When I drove the car in, even the sidelights lit up the inside of the shed to some extent. I looked across through the nearside window. The sacking curtain was still there on its tacks. As far as I could see, it was very much as I had left it. I switched off the engine, took the ignition key out of the lock and turned the lights out. It was as dark as pitch now.

I opened the driving door cautiously until it came up against the wall of the shed. Then I got out and shut the car door. I dropped the ignition key in my pocket. I did not bother to lock the car. I began to feel my way out between the side of the car and the wall of the shed. I could see just a gleam of light from the door, but it was almost as dark outside as it was in. When I got outside, I shut the shed doors, put the hasp back over the staple and turned the key in the lock. Then I stood there, with the bunch of keys in my hand, letting my eyes get used to the darkness.

I do not know exactly when it occurred to me to do what I did. It must have been almost at once, because the whole thing took no time at all. I tiptoed across to the door of the bigger building next door and ran my fingers over the lock. It was much bigger and of a different type. It was a spring cylinder lock, the sort with its keyhole at the bottom. I still could not see much, but I sorted through the keys on the ring with my fingers and found only one key of the right type. I eased it into the lock. It turned smoothly and the lock sprang open. I did not take it off the staple. I guided the bottom of the shank back into the top of the lock and squeezed it in until it came up against the spring lever. Then I left it, hanging on the staple. There must be more of the shank showing than there should be, but I thought you would have to look at it pretty closely to see that it was not locked. Then I walked back over the gravel to the house with the bunch of keys in my hand.

Cynthia came out of the kitchen as I came in at the front door. "All secure," I said. I held the keys out to her, and she took them and dropped them in the pocket of her overall. Then she went past me, as she had before, and turned the key in the front-door lock. It was a routine action. The door had to be locked at night, obviously. It had been locked before and had to be relocked. I might have relocked it myself as I came in, only I had not thought of it. It was only when she had locked it and turned back to me that we saw the symbolism of the thing. We did see it, and at the same moment, just as we had seen the significance of the parting at the stairhead before. Here we were, Cynthia and I, shut in together in this square silent house with our suspicions and our reservations and our almost palpable need of each other. We were both of us too old and too clear-headed not to know what we had on our hands. And intelligent, damn it, since that was the family watchword. I doubt if any two people ever deceived themselves less and each other more than she and I did during my short, extraordinary second stay at Llanglas.

We walked across the hall toward the foot of the stairs. Just before we got there, she turned and went to the back of the hall and switched off all the lights. The lights were still on in the corridor upstairs. She came back and went up the stairs, and I went up behind her. I wanted more than I had ever wanted anything to reach out and take hold of her before we got to the top, but I knew I must not. I knew I must leave the decision to her. I knew what it would be, but I walked up the stairs behind her without touching her, and when we got to the top, she turned right and I turned left, and there we were again with the invisible dividing line between us. There was so obviously nothing to be said, and nothing that needed saying, that I don't think either of us even thought of saying anything. We just stood there for a moment looking at each other. Then she turned and went off along the corridor toward her room. She was already several yards from me when I said, "Good night, Cynthia." She did not pause or turn. She said, "Good night, Mark," and then she went into her room and shut the door behind her. It was the first time anyone in that house had called me by my name. They all knew what it was, but nobody, somehow, had found the need to use it. It was not much, but it was something. I turned and went along to my room. I suppose at some point she must have turned the corridor lights out, because they were out before morning, but I do not know when she did it.

When I woke, there were the gray beginnings of daylight outside, but inside the house there was still hardly enough light to move about by. There was no more sleep left in me, and for a bit I lay staring at the window. From down here on the bed I could see a line of sky over the tops of the hills. It was a clear, faint white. A breeze had got up and covered the silence. I lay for about ten minutes. Then I got up and went to the window. It was still nowhere near fully light, but it was going to be a clear day. The hills were all dark purples against the sky. There was little detail in them. I no longer thought Dick was somewhere up there, but I did not know where he was. I shivered suddenly in the cold air from the window, but I did not want to go back to bed. Instead I came back into the room and started getting dressed.

When I went out into the corridor and shut the door of my room behind me, I was aware at once how quiet the house was. The window of my room had been open, but in the rest of the house they were all shut. This was last night's air and still held last night's silence. I went along the corridor and down the stairs. I went very quietly. If Cynthia was not yet awake, I did not think my movements would wake her. If she had come out of her room in her dressing gown, I should have waited for her at the top of the stairs, full of excitement to see her again. As she did not, there were things I wanted to do. The double edge of my relation with her had its advantages as well as its confusions. I was crossing the hall when it occurred to me to try the door of Merrion's working room. It was not locked. I opened it quietly and put my head inside. I had never been inside the room when I had been here before, but I had seen it through the open door. It did not look very different now, except that it had the relative tidiness of a room not immediately in use. There were plenty of papers about on a pedestal desk and a big table by the wall, but they were lying in trays or gathered into piles with weights on them. The actual working space in the middle of the desk was empty. I shut the door as quietly as I had opened it and went across the hall to the front door.

The air outside was chilly and damp and full of subdued sound. The smell of the autumnal woods was everywhere. It was like so many early mornings at that time of the year. I thought the breeze would die out with sunrise and we should get a clear still day. I walked over toward the shed where my car was. Once I was there, I could not be seen from the house at all. I took one last look back over the gravel and then turned in under the end of the buildings. I lifted the open spring lock off its staple, opened one door of the bigger shed and stepped inside. The thing that struck me at once was the coils of wire rope and the collection of blocks and tackle. It was fairly formidable stuff, and, properly powered, would be up to very heavy loads. What Merrion wanted it for I could not begin to guess. The rest of the stuff was pretty miscellaneous. There was an assortment of hand tools hanging on the wall, and there were, as I had thought, digging tools, picks and shovels and spades. There were also some long iron spikes, with their upper ends spread slightly, as if they had been driven in with a heavy hammer. There was one hammer just inside the door, a seven-pound maul of the sort they use for fencing. The stuff was all clean, but it had been used. I could not answer for the ropes and tackle, but the tools all showed clear signs of wear.

I went outside again and back to the corner of the buildings. There was no sign of movement at the house. I shut the doors of the shed, hung the lock on the staple and pressed the shank down without locking it, as I had the night before. Then I went a few yards off and looked at it. I did not like what I saw. There was far too much shank showing and the lock was too clearly not locked. I went back, took the lock off the staple and opened the door again. Then I went in and looked at the inside of the door. The staple was bolted through the door by a single bolt with a hexagonal nut on the inside. The wood had been drilled to take it, and I reckoned that without the nut the staple would pull out fairly easily. I took an adjustable spanner off the wall and unscrewed the nut. I put the nut down by the wall and went outside again. I was not going to carry the experiment any further at that stage. I had one more look at the house and then went back into the shed again. I took out a spade, the maul and one of the iron spikes and put them down outside. Then I shut the doors, put the lock back over the staple and clicked it home. I picked up the tools and set off into the wood.

I walked thirty or forty yards along the track and turned off right-handed into the trees. Once I was well clear of the track, I put the tools down together at the foot of a tree. Then I went out on to the track again. I thought I could remember the place all right, but to make certain, I took out my knife and cut a small blaze in the bark of the nearest tree, as high as I could conveniently reach. No one would be likely to notice it if he was not looking for it, but I thought I could find it even in the dark if I had a torch with me. I walked another twenty yards in along the track. Then I turned off right-handed again and began to make my way round the back of the house through the edge of the wood.

I must have followed very much the same line as I had once before, after my chance meeting with Ethel Merrion, only this time I did not try to get any distance up on the hill slopes north of the house. I did not mind Cynthia's knowing I had been in the wood. All I wanted was to suggest, if she saw me, that I had gone out and returned on the north side and not on the south, where the locked sheds were. I thought it very likely that she would see me, because both her room and the kitchen faced north, and whether or not she was down by the time I came back, she was not likely to be still asleep. By the time I came out of the wood, the sun was well up, lighting the whole front of the house through the eastern gap in the hills. The wind had gone, as I thought it would, and it was a clear golden day. I was ready to put my early maneuvers out of my mind and concentrate on the pleasure of seeing Cynthia again. If this was double thinking verging on split-mindedness, I make no apology for it. It was no more than the familiar split-mindedness of the married man returning with genuine affection, and even relief, to his wife after a mild extra-marital adventure. There are so many different people in most of us that we cannot let any other person see more than a few of them.

I did in fact look toward the kitchen window as I went past. I thought I saw movement inside, and I noticed at the same time that the curtains of Cynthia's room upstairs were drawn back. Not that this was of much significance. I did not think she was a person to sleep with her curtains drawn, any more than I was. I came in at the front door and went casually across to the sitting room. I found something to read and sat down. I was not acting any part in this. I not only acted, but was, the considerate guest anxious not to let his own early rising disrupt the working of the household.

There were sounds in the kitchen now, and when I heard the door open, I got up and went into the hall to meet her.

We said good morning a little solemnly, but then so we should have anyhow. "Have you been out?" she said. "You must have been up early."

"I was, rather. I couldn't sleep after a bit, and it's a lovely day."

She nodded. "Breakfast in the kitchen," she said. "Do you mind?"

I said, "I'd like it."

We looked at each other in that curious, lost way we did sometimes. Then she said, "Come on, then. It's ready," and I followed her in.

Over breakfast I said, "Does it matter my being here?"

"In what way?"

"Oh—scandal, I suppose. I imagined the village might be interested."

She shook her head. She was genuinely unconcerned. "It doesn't matter to me. I suppose they might be. In fact there's no particular reason why they should know."

"Does nobody come in?"

"To work, you mean? Not when I'm on my own."

"I won't flaunt myself," I said. "There's nothing to take me into the village."

"No. All right. I have to go out occasionally, of course, to shop and so on. But in any case I can't really see it matters."

I said, "That's for you to say."

When we had finished and she got up to clear the things away, I said, "Would you like me to lend a hand?"

"Not really," she said. "It's not much, and I'm better on my own."

"Right," I said. "Then I'll go and make my bed."

"Yes, do that."

I went to the door, but when I got there, I turned, because she was standing still, on the other side of the room, looking after me. "I was wondering," she said. "Would you like to go up on the hills a bit? We could take a meal of sorts. I think—I find it does me good to get out on top of the place occasionally. It's a bit enclosed."

"I wondered whether you didn't feel that. I think I should if I were here all the time. I'd like it very much indeed."

She nodded. "Good. I'll get something ready. Say in about an hour's time?"

"That would be perfect." I turned and went out into the hall and upstairs to straighten my room. I felt as nearly perfectly happy as I had for a very long time. I made no attempt whatever to examine either the quality of my happiness or its justification.

CHAPTER 11

The next time I turned round to look, we were well above the trees, and I could see the whole circle of hills, yellow in the sun, with the wood filling it from side to side. The tops of the trees lay as level as liquid in a bowl. It was all unbelievably symmetrical. Somewhere under the trees the earthwork ran its perfect circle inside the bigger circle of the hills, but there was nothing to show for it from here. Further in still, the abbey had intruded its right-angles into the middle of all this huge circularity, but someone had not allowed the intrusion to last very long. On the extreme western edge of the earthwork, as far as possible from the end of the tarmac road, I knew that someone, quite recently, had started digging into it, but had covered up his work, so that in a few more months the disturbance would no longer show.

Merrion was a medievalist, whose proper interest was the abbey, and who seemed to resent the suggestion that the earthwork might be as old as it looked. Dick, who would have been on to it like a terrier on a rat-hole —Dick had been here, but Merrion said they had not even discussed it. Dick was still somewhere hereabouts, but no longer in a position to argue the point. Merrion said Dick had died up on the high hills, but that was not true either. And Cynthia, who knew a lot about Merrion, whatever she knew about Dick—Cynthia was standing just behind me in the quiet sunshine, looking out as I was across the whole huge saucer of Llanglas. All we wanted, both of us, was to be at peace up here, just for the day, and to forget the whole damned place. I turned, and she took her eyes off the circle of the hills and looked at me instead. She said, "Shall we go up higher?"

"Yes," I said, "let's go a lot higher." She nodded and turned and started to climb again, and I climbed after her. It was not climbing in any strict sense. We followed a sheep track that dodged up from patch to patch of greenery between the projecting ribs of rock. It was no more than strenuous walking. It had us both a bit out of breath, but the air was worth breathing, even a little noisily. She was one of the few women I knew who could have worn trousers with any degree of assurance, but to my relief she preferred a skirt. I watched her going up ahead of me as I had watched her going upstairs. There was no self-conscious grace about it, but every movement was worth watching.

We halted twice more, to look back and get our breath, and then we came out on to a broad grassy shelf with a steep rock face above and below it and all the world at our feet. She stopped and said, "Here, I thought. High enough?"

I looked down from the edge of the shelf and she came and stood beside me. The saucer full of trees had dropped back to a deep hollow in the vast panorama of hills. The bare rocky peaks, where the real climbing began, were all along the western sky. "High enough," I said. "Do you always come here?"

"Generally," she said.

"But generally alone?"

"Always alone. Until now."

"Why now, then?"

She turned and sat down on the grass, gathering her skirt round her knees and leaning back against the wall of rock. I unslung the haversack and put it down. Then I went and sat down beside her.

"I don't know," she said. "I really don't know. I'm a bit out of my depth altogether."

I said, "Never mind. Forget it. The important thing is that you've brought me here, and here we are. And it's all—" I waved a hand comprehensively at everything that lay below us—"it's all a long way down." She nodded. She was not looking at me. I said, "Have you never thought of leaving it and getting away?"

"Not permanently. I go away sometimes, of course. But I've always liked it here. And Roger needs someone to look after the place."

"I don't see why he should rely on you," I said. "Especially now."

She turned her head sharply and looked at me. "Why now?" she said. We were sitting almost shoulder to shoulder, and when we both turned, our faces were very close. There was challenge in her eyes when she turned, but the closeness was too much for both of us. The color crept up under her skin, and the long, firm mouth drooped a little.

I said, "Now he's married, I mean," but I said it without really thinking about it. My voice came huskily from a suddenly dry mouth.

She said, "Oh, that." It was hardly more than a whisper.

"You're so beautiful," I said, but she jerked her head away from me, as suddenly and decisively as if she was snapping a thread between us. Then she gathered her feet under her and got up and went over to the haversack.

"Come on," she said. "Let's eat."

I said, "Yes, of course. Let's eat." I did not mind. We had the whole day before us, and we were up here on the roof of the world. I could wait. We ate cheerfully, and a very good meal it was, sharpened by the golden air and the curious, ineradicable savor of the successful picnic. When we had finished, she put the things back into the haversack and took it back to where I had first put it down, close to the edge of the shelf. I went after her, and for a moment or two we both knelt there, looking down. Then I turned and put my arms round her and forced her gently down on the grass. When I kissed her, her arms came up round my neck, and we made a much better job of it than we had the first time. We neither of us said anything. We just went on kissing. But when my hand began to wander over her body, she took her mouth away and said, "I don't know. I don't think I'm very good at this sort of thing."

I said, "Not enough experience?"

"No experience at all. Do you mind?"

"Of course I don't mind. Only you must let me teach you."

She said, "Not—not too much. Not now. Please."

"All right," I said, "not now. I can wait."

For a very long time after that we said nothing. We just lay together on the grass, and the sun moved more than we did. At the end of it all she said suddenly, "Why did it have to be you?"

"I don't know," I said. "Does it matter?"

"I think it does, rather. I think we'd better go down now."

"All right. Let's go down."

The sun was well over toward the west and dropping down to the hills. For all the golden weather, the days were getting very short. The mist was gathering in the valley as we came down into it. When we got under the level of the trees, we walked into the dusk, and when we came to the house, it looked very dark. I stood in the hall while she went round turning on lights. When she came back into the hall, I said, "Cynthia, won't you come away from this place?"

She had started to go up the stairs, but now she stopped and turned round and looked at me. "I can't," she said. "Not yet. You do understand that?"

I understood it, or thought I did. For the matter of that, I knew I could not go either, not even if I was taking Cynthia with me. "Yes," I said, "all right. But some time?"

She said very seriously, "I hope so. But you must give me time." Then she turned and went on upstairs.

Later over supper she said, "How much did Dick mean to you?"

I thought about this. I wanted to be sure I got it right. Then I said, "Not much, once we were both grown up. Very little, perhaps. I mean, so long as he was alive."

She was sitting opposite me across the kitchen table, with her elbows on the table and her chin resting on her hands, looking up at me with her great gray eyes from under her dark brows. She suddenly reminded me of her brother, looking at me like that. Generally she did not remind me of him at all, despite the obvious likeness. Now there was something, a touch of his watchfulness and calculation. She said, "And now he's dead?"

"More," I said. "It's difficult to say why."

She dropped her eyes and for a moment stared down at the table. Then she nodded and got up.

That night when we separated at the head of the stairs, we did not kiss. I knew we should not, and we did not. Kissing had been fine in the sunlight up on the hill, but in this dark house it would not do. So we said good-night and went off, each to our own end of the corridor. Before she got to her door she said, "I'll have to go out in the morning. Will you be all right?"

"I'll be all right," I said. She nodded and went into her room. When I got into my room, I could hear that the wind was getting up outside, and before long there was rain driving against the window. The golden weather was over, and I wondered how we were going to get on without it.

By next day the rain had stopped, but it was dark weather and much colder. Cynthia got her car out and went off after breakfast. "I'll be back in time to get lunch," she said. "You can brew coffee if you want it, can't you?"

"I can," I said. "Don't worry. I really am very capable of looking after myself."

I said it smiling, but she looked at me seriously. "I know," she said. Then she went out to her car, and I heard it move off over the gravel. When it had gone, I walked across the hall and turned the handle of the door of Merrion's work room. It was locked. I stood there with my hand still on the handle, turning it this way and that and trying the door, as if I could not quite believe it. I could feel my heart beating. Then a thought occurred to me, and I went out of the house and across to the shed where the tools were kept. I think I almost ran. I took hold of the staple, with the hasp locked over it, and tried to ease it away from the door. It shifted at once. Not much, but enough to make it certain that no one had put the nut back on the inside of the door. A tremendous surge of relief swept over me. I did not want to get into the shed, not then. I had the tools I wanted already out in the wood. It was just that I could not bear the thought that Cynthia had found out what I had done. The locking of Merrion's door might or might not be an act of war of a sort. There were other, more innocent, explanations. But even if it was, it was an act on her part. What I could not bear was her knowing that I had acted first. I did not mind her mistrusting me nearly so much when I knew that she had no concrete reason for doing so. I know this was no more reasonable than half the other things I did and felt during those few days. I can only say that this was what I did feel.

I went back to the house and got a mackintosh. I did not trust the weather too far. Then I set out along the track into the wood. When I came to the blaze on the tree, I turned off and picked up the spade and the iron-sounding spike. I left the hammer where it was. The tools were all rusted slightly, and I made a mental note that at some point I must clean them before I put them back. I did not know when this would be. I did not know what was going to happen at all. I draped the mackintosh over one shoulder and put the tools over the other, and walked on into the wood. When I came to the gap in the earthwork, I turned up on to it and went the way I had gone before. I did not know my way through the middle of the wood, and could not be sure of hitting the earthwork at the point I wanted if I tried to walk straight across to it. Also, now that I knew a bit more what I was after, I thought I might see more signs of disturbance at other points. I did not, in fact, see anything until I had almost reached the place I was making for, and had crossed the ditch to the level ground on the far side. What I saw then was a small round hole close to the edge of the ditch. It was a thing I was bound to miss the first time. Even if I had seen it, I should probably have thought it an animal's burrow of some sort. Now I put the point of my iron spike into the hole and pushed it gently in. It fitted the hole exactly and went straight in for perhaps eighteen inches. Then it came up against something hard and would go no further. I pulled the spike out and walked on. I saw no more holes until I came to the stretch where the whole surface had been disturbed. I did not know what it meant. I knew somebody had been sounding the edge of the ditch with the spike, but I did not know what they had been looking for.

When I came to the place, I put down my mackintosh and the tools against a tree growing halfway down the inner slope of the ditch. Then I went back up on to the top and stood there, looking at it. From what I could see, I thought that for a stretch perhaps twelve or fifteen feet long the whole top soil had been dug out and then replaced. A certain amount of turf was in position, and the whole thing was covered with a fresh drift of leaves, but between them the surface of the earth was still very slightly granular and uneven. On both sides of this stretch, from the point where I was standing, there were signs of disturbance, but the original surface was still in place. There were more spike holes here, and dents and shallow furrows, as if heavy things had been moved about, but no systematic digging. I walked clear of the whole area of disturbance and then turned and went slowly back, not looking at the earth under my feet. Now that I was expecting it, there was no mistaking the new surface when I came to it. The soil had been well tamped down, and it had settled naturally since, but it still gave under the foot. I went on and after a few yards felt the harder surface under me again. After a bit I looked down to see where I had got to. I saw the dent at once. A perfect right angle is the most man-made of things. I stooped and brushed the leaves away. There was a fairly deep rectangular depression in the turf, as if something very heavy had been there for quite a while. It was four or five feet each way. There were small patches of loose soil in and round it, but over most of the area the turf was hard and compressed. It was almost at the end of the whole disturbed stretch. A yard or two beyond it there was nothing more to be seen.

I went back and collected the iron spike. Then I started moving again, very slowly, over the disturbed soil. After every few feet I stopped, lifted the spike shoulder-high and drove it down into the top of the bank. It was heavy in itself, and I put a good deal of force behind it. Even so, it did not go in more than six or eight inches until I got to the new surface. Then it went in a foot or more before the friction of the soil stopped it. This happened twice. The third time it struck something under the surface. The thing was completely rigid and impermeable, and the shock jolted the bones of my hands and wrists and loosened my grip on the spike, so that it keeled over sideways in the soft soil. I pulled it out and went on again, probing more cautiously now. For another ten feet or so the hard thing was there, about fifteen inches under the surface. Then I was into soft soil again.

I went back again, probing out sideways from the center line, until I had the thing fairly clearly demarcated. I reckoned it was about twelve feet long and four or five feet wide. I could not guess how deep it went. There was soft soil, the soft soil of the new surface, all round it. I put the spike down and went back for the spade. It did not take long. I opened up a hole a yard across and the necessary fifteen inches deep. The bottom of the hole was solid rock. It was not masonry. It was one continuous face of rock, and even under the clinging remains of the top soil it looked rough and weather-worn. It reminded me of something I had seen recently, but I could not think what. All I knew was that it could not be natural. For God knows what reason, there was a huge stone embedded in the earth at this point, and someone, not very long ago, had uncovered it and then covered it up again. I shoveled the top soil back into the hole and trampled it well down. Then, just in case, I smoothed the surface over as best I could and scattered leaves over it.

I took the spade and spike back to where I had first put them down with my mackintosh. Then I sat down to think. I did not know enough to get very far. I did not know what the stone was or what it was doing there. All I knew was that someone had located it, as I had, by probing for it with the spike, and had then been sufficiently interested to uncover it completely. The busy digging brought the professor's phrase into my head.

Like a terrier at a rat-hole, he had said. I knew then that this was Dick's work. Whatever the stone was, it was nothing to do with the abbey, any more than the earthwork was the monks' perimeter wall. It was something older, much, much older, and it was the thing, or one of the things, which had brought Dick to Llanglas. I still did not know what had happened or where Dick was, but I knew that Merrion had lied and lied again.

I had made myself hot with my digging, but now the air struck cold as I sat there, and I shivered suddenly and violently. I got up and put my mackintosh on. There was not much warmth in it, but it was better than nothing. I did not think there was anything more I could do here. I left the spade and spike where they were and walked once more the length of the disturbed patch on the edge of the ditch. I had just got to the far end when I heard something moving in the bushes at the bottom of the ditch. It was a stealthy, continuous sound, as if something was making its way through the thick undergrowth. I stood there peering toward the sound, but there was nothing to be seen, only the thicket that came up to the foot of the bank, with the trunks of the trees rising out of it. The sound went on, a faint but continuous rustle. I did not really think, even from the first, that it was anything human. A man could not move as steadily as that through the tangle at the foot of the bank. I wanted to make sure, but I did not feel the need for any particular caution. I went straight down the slope and forced my way into the thicket. I think the sound stopped as soon as I moved. I cannot be certain, because what happened next put it completely out of my head. I never saw what it was that made the sound. Perhaps a badger. The wood was quiet enough for them to come out in daylight. All I know is that I forced my way between two bushes and almost fell over the winch.

It was an extremely powerful hand winch, fully geared. It lay on its side, with its wooded base up-ended toward me. For a split second my eyes took in the solid rectangle of timber, and then I had the connection my mind was groping for. It was the winch that had made that deep indentation on the inner edge of the ditch. It had stood there for some time. Then it had been maneuvered to the edge and simply rolled down. I could see the marks on the bank now, when I came to look for them. Whether it had simply rolled under the bushes or whether it had been dragged under them I did not know. At any rate, it was quite invisible from the top. If it had been deliberately hidden, the job had been well done.

There was nothing with it, but I remembered the unexplained wire ropes and tackle I had seen in the tool shed. They needed no explanation now. There was only one explanation of the whole thing. Someone had not been content merely to unearth the stone. They had had it in mind to lift it. Whether they had even made the attempt I could not tell. They would have needed some sort of lifting device, probably the tripod of heavy timbers we call a gyn. If the stone was no bigger downward than it was sideways and the tackle was properly rigged round it, I reckoned the winch would have been up to the job. But I had no evidence that it had been used.

I pulled myself back from between the bushes and let them close over the thing they were hiding. I went back up and picked up the spade and spike. I was really cold now, chilled through physically and in some way mentally. There was too much here I did not understand. I set out with a sort of brisk desperation on the walk home.

CHAPTER 12

When I came to the track, I went with a good deal of caution. I did not know how long Cynthia would be away. If she got back and found me not at home, it was just possible that she might walk into the wood on the chance of meeting me. She would know I was not out on the road and, as I have said, short of climbing the hillsides, there were only the two ways to go. I kept the tools close to my side and my eyes well ahead, ready to jettison my contraband in the bushes if I saw any signs of movement. I could of course have hidden them at any point, but my instinct was to put them back with the hammer if I could and then, when the opportunity offered, return all three to the shed. I did not see what further use I had for them.

In fact I saw nothing and met no one before I got to my blaze on the tree. Then I turned off into the wood and put the spade and spike down where they had been before. I turned and made my way out through the bushes, moving with less caution now. When I came out on to the track, I found old Evans coming to meet me from the direction of the house. He was no more than a dozen yards from me. There was no chance of missing him.

At least he looked as startled as I was, but we both

kept on walking until we were almost face to face in the track. Then we both stopped. He was in his walking-out clothes. He looked as much of an animated scarecrow as ever, but he was not actively horrifying. He said, "Oh—" It was a very deep, rumbling sound, of the sort an angry animal makes before it has made up its mind what it wants to do. I measured him up, quite consciously, with my eyes and decided that in physical terms I could deal with him if I had to. All the same, the last thing I wanted was to touch him. Then he said, "Mr. Hawkins, is it?" exactly as he had the first time. I did not say anything. "Come back, is it?" he said. It occurred to me that he had not expected, after our last encounter, that I should ever have the courage to go into the wood again. I may have been wrong in this, but the mere suggestion of this sort of malicious calculation in him gave me a whiff of angry confidence. Also, I suppose I was a bit ashamed, now I had met him again, of the way I had behaved before, and this made me angry too.

"That's right," I said. "You too, Mr. Evans?"

This made him angry, as it was meant to. His mouth worked and his dark eyes opened wide and stared at me. "Me come back?" he said. "Always here, I am. I've a right to be here, see? Once there was many of us, now there's only me, but the right is there, just the same. I don't know about you, Mr. Hawkins. Perhaps Mr. Merrion invited you, like, perhaps not. I don't know, see?"

I did not like this at all, but I was not going to make it worse by arguing with him. Instead I said, "What about my brother, then?"

Once more he repeated himself from our first meeting. "Him that's dead?" he said. "He came here with Mr. Merrion, right enough. Very friendly he was with him." He suddenly smiled his wide, ghastly smile. "And with Mrs. Merrion, too," he said. "But at first it was all him and Mr. Merrion. Thick as thieves, they was, poking about on the round and measuring and making notes and all. It was later they quarreled."

I could feel my heart thumping steadily against my ribs as I stood there, but I looked at the old horror with a show of mildly amused interest. I did not know which question to ask first.

"On the round?" I said. I thought I knew what he meant, but I had to make sure.

"That's right," he said. He jerked his head toward the wood over my shoulder. "Up on top of the round they was, poking and prodding at it. I saw them. Not from near, mind you, but I saw them."

I said, "Poking about? What would they be looking for?"

He looked at me. He had stopped smiling now. He looked very cunning, with the sort of grotesque, self-satisfied cunning of the ill-disposed child. "That I'm not saying," he said, but I did not think he knew. "Things better left, I reckon. All better left, it is. What do they want to go poking about for?"

I nodded. "And then they quarreled?" I said, and suddenly he smiled again. I was getting to know the kind of thing that amused him.

"That's right. Proper old quarrel they had. Shouting at him, Mr. Merrion was, going on something terrible."

Something in the way he said it gave me the clue. I said, "But you didn't hear what he was saying?"

He shook his head. He looked suddenly crestfallen, too crestfallen even to pretend with me. "I don't hear well," he said. "Not at a distance, like. I hear you well enough, when it's just you and me talking. But not at a distance, and with the wind there was blowing." Then he brightened up. "But real angry he was, Mr. Merrion. You could see that. Well, he would be, I reckon, with your brother going on the way he was."

I knew he was going to smile again, and he did. Expecting it did not make it look any better. Nevertheless,

I walked up to him, and passed him quite close, and went on a few paces in the direction of the house. Then I stopped and turned. He did not smell at all, or at least not of any sort of corruption. There was a faint whiff of something unusual about him, but he was not dirty, nor were his clothes, which are usually the trouble. When I turned, he had half-turned too, but only half, so that he was looking at me almost over his shoulder.

He did not like my going past him like this. He was angry again. He said, "What do you want to come here for? You won't do any good here. You keep away, see?"

I nodded. "I'm going," I said. I turned and started off toward the house.

"That's right," he said. "You go off now. Waiting for you, Miss Merrion will be." I knew with a nasty certainty that he was smiling again, but I did not turn round to see.

Whether Cynthia was in fact waiting for me I cannot say. She was there when I got in, but she was still busy in the kitchen, and I did not think she had been in very long. When I came to the kitchen door, she said, "Hullo. Been out?"

I nodded and sat myself on the edge of the table. "I met old Evans," I said.

She stopped doing whatever it was she was doing and came and stood in front of me. "In the wood?" she said.

"Not very far in, in fact. Pretty close to the house."

She was looking at me very intently. I thought she too must be remembering my last encounter with him. I had not mentioned him then, but she must have known. She said, "He's mad, of course."

I thought about this. "Only north-northwest," I said, "and that's not a common quarter for the wind in these parts. Most of the time I reckon he's sane enough. Clever, if it comes to that. He's—I don't know, a devotee, I suppose, would you call it that? Most of us are devotees of some sort. We can be crazy enough if the wind's right."

She would not have this at all. "No, no," she said. "Not as crazy as that. It's a sort of local lunacy, do you see?"

"I have an idea, but I may be wrong. You tell me."

"We don't really know, of course. It's the sort of thing you never do know, not properly. You pick up fragments and piece them together as best you can. Only old Evans could really tell you, and he won't. But there's a long tradition of—something in the wood. Rites, observances, pagan vestigia—you know the kind of thing."

I said, "It sounds like witchcraft."

"I don't know about that. If there was witchcraft in these parts, it probably got mixed up with it. But I think it was something strictly local. There's the abbey, of course."

I said, "There was the abbey, but someone succeeded in destroying it. If you ask me, they've been celebrating ever since."

She gave me a very long, penetrating look. It was neither friendly nor hostile, merely speculative. Then she said, "You've got too much imagination for an engineer."

"That's what your brother said, more or less. But I'm right, aren't I? Old Evans is the last flicker of a long tradition. He said so himself, or almost. I can't remember exactly what he did say, but he knows, all right. The abbey, all those centuries ago, was an intrusion, only the thing it intruded on then was still very much alive. It wasn't just a crazy old man the monks took on, it was a whole obsessed countryside. And they weren't strong enough, not in the long run. Or that's as I read it."

She said, "They lasted quite a long time. Roger says a hundred years at least."

"So they may have. But it wasn't long enough to kill the other thing, not completely. God knows how long that had been there when the monks moved in, and it has lasted, one way or another—what?—six or seven hundred years after the last monk was thrown out and the last stone knocked over. It may have got a bit rusty while the abbey was there. It would never have got back to what it was before the monks came. But they weren't going to kill it in a mere hundred years, not a thing like that. I suppose old Evans really is the last of it. There's still the stone. It could make its own devotees, don't you think?"

"You've seen the stone?"

"Of course I've seen it. I've felt it, too. That was there long before the abbey, wasn't it?"

She nodded. "They squared it up and incorporated it in some sort of gatehouse. They probably had a chapel *ad portas*. They thought that would—tame it, I suppose."

"It's been tried before. Only here it didn't work. The abbey is down and the stone is still there." Something in my mind was trying to attract my attention, but I was busy watching Cynthia. It was only when she turned away and went on with whatever she was doing that I made the connection. I knew now what it was that the buried stone had reminded me of. It was the standing stone by the track. There were two stones, one standing and one buried, but they were the same sort of stone and, unless I was mistaken, both weathered in the same sort of way. I did not know at all what it meant, but I did not think that the buried stone had always been buried.

Cynthia said, "What's the matter?" She was standing by the door looking at me, and I was still half on and half off the kitchen table, looking at nothing but two stones in my mind's eye.

I looked up at her. "I was thinking," I said, and she came over to me suddenly and took hold of my hands. Her face was full of distress.

"Don't," she said. "Don't, please. It won't do any good. It's all done with now."

I stood up and put my arms round her, and for a moment or two we clung to each other, as if for comfort. But even so my mind went on working. "I'll try not to," I said. "Perhaps—do you think I'd better go away, after all?"

She caught her breath when I said it, but whatever it had been her instinct to say, she did not say it. Instead her mind, as so often, took control. She thought, her face turned down and away from me. Then she said, "I think perhaps you should. Only not now. Tomorrow, perhaps." She looked up, and we looked at each other for quite a long time before I kissed her.

"All right," I said. "We'll decide tomorrow." I kissed her once more, very gently, and then she took herself away from me. "There's one thing," I said. "Does it matter old Evans having seen me? I mean, his knowing I'm here? I don't think he liked my being here."

She said, "He doesn't like any of us being here. But I don't think it matters, no. He's an old crackpot, but I don't think he's the sort to make trouble." She was quite sure about this. She had said the same thing about me. She was wrong, as it happened, in both cases, but she had no doubts at all.

"That's all right, then," I said. "All the same, I think I'd better not stay too long. You still don't know when your brother will be back?"

"Yes. Yes, I heard from him today. Not for another week, he says."

I nodded. "That's all right, then. I'll be gone long before then."

She said, "Yes, you'll be gone."

There was such desolation in her voice that I said, "I don't want to go. You know that."

"I know that." She said it with a sudden, rather disconcerting touch of impatience. "But I think you'd better, all the same."

We ate a rather silent lunch later, and after that I did not see her for the rest of the day. I do not know where she went. I think out walking on the hills by herself, as I fancied she did very often when she was alone here. I did not see her go, but I knew she was not in the house. There is no mistaking the feel of an empty house, especially a house like this one. All the same, I looked for her everywhere except at her end of the corridor. I could not go there, but I knew I should not find her if I did.

When I really made up my mind to the fact, I went and sat in the sitting room. I did not want to go out again. I sat for half an hour or more. Then I got up and went across the hall and tried the door of Merrion's room. It was still locked. I went into the kitchen, looking for a place where keys might be kept. That first evening she had brought the garage keys from the kitchen. There had been nothing on that bunch which would open the mortice lock of a door, but people generally keep keys all together if they do not leave them in the locks. The kitchen window commanded the whole north side of the house. If she came in from that side, I should see her long before she got near the house. If she came in from the other side, I should at least hear her come in at the front door. I shut the kitchen door most of the way, so that you could not see into the kitchen from the hall, but I could hear anything there was to hear. Then I got out things for making tea and put a kettle on the stove. It was much too early for tea, but there was no reason why I should not make myself a cup if I felt like it. Then I started to search.

It took me no time at all, in fact. I do not think she had ever considered the possibility of systematic ferreting. For all I know, even now, she may never have had me in mind at all when she locked the door of Merrion's room. At any rate, I found the keys, all together, in a drawer under some folded tablecloths. It did not look as if they had been put there specially. That was where they were kept. I had Merrion's door open less than five minutes after I went into the kitchen. The room looked very much as I had seen it before the door was locked. I did not know what I was looking for or how much time I had. I decided to give myself five minutes in case there was anything to be found.

I went back into the kitchen. I took the kettle off the stove and emptied it, put the tea things away and put all the keys back in the drawer under the linen. Then I went straight across to Merrion's room and shut myself in. Even if Cynthia came in while I was there, I saw no reason why she should try a door she had left locked. With any luck at all I should be able to get out of the room unseen and get the door locked later, perhaps when she was upstairs. But I had much rather I was out and the door locked again before she came in. I looked at my watch to see when my five minutes would be up. Then I went to work.

The first thing I found was that all the drawers of the desk were locked except two, and they held nothing but stationery. There was nothing I could do about that. The key or keys would be with Merrion at Bristol, not under the tablecloths in the kitchen. That left only the papers on the desk and table. There were quite a lot of them, but it did not take me long to see if they were of any interest. None of them on the desk was. The papers on the table looked even less hopeful. They looked like things Merrion had put aside rather than kept ready for reference. There was a lot of mimeographed stuff, minutes of meetings, copies of papers given by other people, even some programs and agenda papers. There was a small pile of printed journals and a sheaf of press clippings. It was all the sort of stuff you put aside with the honorable intention of reading it when you have time. I had just given it up for useless when I saw the two sheets clipped together, just showing out of the top of one of the journals. They looked as if they might have been used as a marker and then forgotten. When I pulled them out, I saw that they were in Dick's writing. The top one contained a few lines of writing. It looked like a quotation with an ascription underneath. I say it looked like, because of all things in the world, it was in Latin.

I count myself a reasonably educated man for a member of my profession, but I cannot pretend that I can whip the meaning out of four lines of Latin, nor can I memorize them in a matter of seconds. I had seen James Bond memorize his instructions in films and then, with rather self-conscious virtue, burn them with his cigarette lighter, but I do not believe he ever had them in Latin. All the same, the first word was enough to set my heart going even faster than it was. *Lapides.* Stones. Whatever it was, it was something to do with stones, and that in itself was enough to make it interesting. The second sheet had only two short lines of writing, including figures.

I had to have more time, and there was only one thing to do. I put the papers in my pocket, went to the door and opened it quietly. There was no one about. I went out and shut the door behind me. Then I fairly ran for my room. I pulled out pencil and paper, sat down at the dressing table and copied both papers exactly. I did not try at that stage to get any sense out of them. I concentrated on getting them down correctly. Then I put the originals back in my pocket and ran downstairs again.

When I was in Merrion's room with the door shut behind me, I realized that I did not know which of the journals the papers had been in, still less at what page. I could only hope that Merrion, if he found them, would not remember either. In any case, it was a risk

I had to take. I put them back in the middle of a journal at what looked about the right place in the pile. Then I went out of the room and shut the door behind me.

I went into the kitchen again. There was no time for play-acting with the tea things. I took the key out of the drawer, went back to Merrion's room, locked the door and went back to the kitchen again. Here I had to take more care. I arranged the keys in the drawer as nearly as possible as they had been when I found them, and put the tablecloths back over them. I was out in the hall again when I saw Cynthia through one of the windows beside the door. She was coming across the gravel toward the door. I could not tell which side of the house she had come from. The kitchen window faced north and Merrion's room south, but I did not think I could have been seen from outside through either of them. In any case, she was walking slowly, head down, and looked preoccupied. I was standing in the middle of the hall when she opened the door and came in.

"Hullo," I said. "I wondered where you were. Have you been out?"

CHAPTER 13

Lapides quoque, quos in ruinosis locis et silvestribus daemonum ludificationibus decepti venerantur, ubi et vota vovent et deferunt, funditus effodiantur, atque in tali loco proiciantur, ubi nunquam a cultoribus suis inveniri possint.

I had quite enjoyed my Latin at school. I never got to the point of finding out if there was anything written in it worth reading. From what I knew of the Romans, I found it difficult to believe there was. Great engineers, some of them, but not oversensitive. But I had enjoyed the unraveling and reassembling of a fully inflected language, and I had been quite good at it before I turned aside after things like stresses and strains and the theory of moments. Now, with a curiously automatic revival of old habits, I ran quickly through my piece of translation to see if there were any totally unfamiliar words I was likely to get hung up on. There did not seem to be. I did not like the look of *funditus* much, but all the *fund-* words had something to do with founding. I went back to the beginning and started to construe.

Lapides quoque, quos—The stones also which—*in ruinosis locis et silvestribus*—in ruinous and wooded places. I was suddenly gripped by an enormous excitement. I had never tried to describe Llanglas in a phrase, but if it was not a ruinous and wooded place, I did not know what it was. I went on, a bit more laboriously now. *Quos*—which—was the object, and I wanted a subject and a verb. *Decepti* would do for a nominative plural, and *venerantur* for a verb. It looked like a passive, but if it was going to govern *quos*, it would have to have an active meaning. The Romans, or somebody, had a word for verbs like that, only I could not remember what it was. *Quos decepti venerantur*, then. Which deceived people venerate. Then the words before *decepti* dropped into place: they went with it. *Daemonum* was a genitive, because the nominative was *daemones*. *Daemonum ludificationibus decepti.* Deceived by the ludifications of demons. Ludifications was not a real word. Sport? Delusions, perhaps. People deceived by the delusions of demons. I thought of old Evans, naked and rigid in the moonlight, prancing about in the wood. Cynthia had said, "He's mad, of course," and I had disputed this. Perhaps I had been right. Old Evans was not mad. He was merely deceived by demons.

I went on. *Ubi et vota vovent et deferunt. Et—et.* Both—and. Where they both vow vows and—*deferunt?* Defer? Worship, perhaps? Sacrifice? Anyway, something of the sort. Where they vow vows (or make offerings?) and worship. That was the end of the subordinate clauses that went with *lapides*. Now for a main verb. There were two, in fact. *Effodiantur* and, further on, *proiciantur*. Passives again. And—aha!—subjunctives. Think I don't know a subjunctive when I see one? Subjunctives as the main verbs meant an exhortation or command of some sort. *Fodio* meant dig, so *effodio* would mean dig out. Let them be dug out. I could take *funditus* in my stride now. If it was an adverb, it was a funny one, but it could have only one meaning. From the foundations, from the bottom. Let them be dug out from the foundations. *Atque proiciantur.* And let them be projected, thrown away. *In tali loco* was easy. In such a place. Then *ubi* would go with it. In such a place where— The rest came in one piece. *Ubi nunquam a cultoribus suis inveniri possint.* Where they can never be found by their *cultores. Cultor* meant a cultivator, but here, obviously, a worshipper, the follower of a cult.

I went back over my disjointed scribblings. Then I wrote it all out in one piece, embellishing it a bit, but keeping what I was certain was the general sense. I wrote, "The stones, too, which those deceived by the deluding of demons venerate in ruinous and wooded places, at which they worship and make offerings, let these be rooted out utterly and cast away in a place where they can never be found by their worshippers." Underneath was written, in Dick's rather florid but still scholarly hand, "Council of Nantes, c. 896 A.D." I did not know what the Council of Nantes was, but the voice of embattled Christendom was unmistakable. I imagined the early medieval church, still almost in the fringe of the Dark Ages, making its plans for the subjugation of a Europe nominally Christian but still seething with paganism just under the surface. If old Evans, more than a thousand years later, still danced by moonlight round the standing stone in the wood, the things that went on at the time of the Council of Nantes may well have worried the fathers of the church.

I wondered how long the uprooting of the neolithic sanctuaries had gone on. The monks would have come to Llanglas two or three hundred years after the Council of Nantes. Had they still been at it? Here, it was true, the stone had not been cast down and hidden. It had been left standing and sanctified instead. Only the sanctification had not stuck. Whatever the monks had made of it, it had been the stone of the dancing man a hundred years later, and still was. Then I remembered the other stone buried by the ditch. I knew it had not always been underground. I wondered if perhaps that one at least had been buried to put it out of the way of old Evans' ancestors. But even if the monks had buried it, they would not have taken it up to the lip of the ditch first. It must have been there already, probably standing on end, like the dancing man's stone on the track. All they would have needed to do was to dig a big enough hole alongside it and then topple it in and cover it up. After another century of ecclesiastical supervision, its lurking presence would have been forgotten, even by the early Evanses. Also, if anyone remembered it was there, they would probably not have stood it up again. It needed a more enlightened age for that, an age more interested in the tremendous cultures of the second millennium before Christ than in the ludifications of medieval demons. Also, I thought, it needed a winch.

The other note was not in Latin, but that did not make it any easier to understand. It read:

Interval av. 36′ as Av. outer circle?
Total prob. nearly 200, cf. Av. 100.

I took it to mean "Interval may average 36 ft., like average of outer circle. Total probably nearly 200, as compared with average of 100." But I did not know at all what the intervals might be between, or what it was that totaled two hundred instead of the expected hundred. I think I noticed the two capital A's. I must have, because of what happened afterwards. But I did not have a chance to think the thing out, because Cynthia called "Mark!" from along the corridor. I bundled the papers into the top drawer of the dressing table and went to the door.

She was standing at the top of the stairs, and my heart turned over at the sight of her. She had been utterly withdrawn during the early part of the evening, as if her mind was still occupied with whatever it was she had been thinking about on her walk. We had talked very little, and she had hardly met my eye. When she had gone into the kitchen to get the supper, I had gone up to my room, as I was longing to do, to see what I could make of Dick's notes. I did not hear her come upstairs, but she must have finished in the kitchen and then gone along to her room. Now she was transformed.

She stood there very straight, smiling a little. She had a very plain dark dress on. Her hair was piled up on top of her head, and her eyes, always the dominant feature, looked so enormous that I thought she must have been doing something to them. She said, "Supper's ready. Are you?" Her voice was not quite steady.

I walked very slowly toward her along my half of the corridor, never taking my eyes off her. "I'm ready," I said. When I reached her, she turned, and we went downstairs side by side. When we got to the bottom, she stopped and turned to face me.

She said, "You are going tomorrow, aren't you?" I was right, she had been doing something to her eyes and more than usual to her mouth. It was very well done. Enormous complications of pleasure welled up in my mind. I was pleased that this wonderful, rather austere woman could do herself up like a teenage typist when the mood took her. I was pleased that, when she did, she should do it with such artistry and assurance. I was pleased, obviously and simply, that she should do it for my benefit. Whether I was pleased at her question and its implication I did not know. I knew two things. I knew that she wanted me to say yes, and I knew that when she looked at me like that, I could not say anything else. But I wondered why she did and why it seemed to mean so much to her. All this time I was looking into that upturned, beautiful, bedizened face, almost daring it to keep up its appeal until I made up my mind to answer. I believe that, as so often, she saw through the dare and made her own evaluation of it, because suddenly the wide eyes narrowed and the tense mouth twitched into something like a smile. I smiled too. I could not help it. "All right," I said, "I'm going tomorrow."

She whirled away from me at once, heading for the kitchen. "That's right," she said. She sounded as pleased as Punch, like a calculating little girl who has got her way with a difficult and reluctant daddy. I followed her. I did not know what to think. The truth is, I did not want to think at all. All I wanted was to fall in with her suddenly festive mood and let tomorrow look after itself. Her mood was outrageously festive and she made the whole occasion a festive one. We ate in the kitchen as we always did, but the meal was special, and she had got out a bottle of Merrion's wine, which I had not seen since I came back to Llanglas. Nothing, after a bit, seemed to matter at all but our reciprocal delight in each other's company.

Usually, and by agreement, I left her when the meal was finished, and went into the sitting room while she tidied up. Tonight I could not. I sat, as I had sat only that morning, half on and half off the kitchen table, with the remains of a glass of wine in my hand, watching her while she went about her job. She had to my knowledge drunk her fair share of the bottle, but it seemed, at least in my eyes, only to increase her grace and sure-handedness. She looked at me every now and then, and smiled, but she did not send me away. She did not speak. She went on with what she was doing, playing with a sort of innocent but consummate assurance to her gallery of one. At last, when everything else was done, she came and held out her hand. She said, "Can I have your glass?"

I drank the little that was left in it and held it out to her. "All that I have is yours," I said. She bowed and took the glass, which was not mine anyway, and washed it under the tap and put it with the rest of the things.

"Now go and sit down while I make the coffee," she said.

I did not want to go, still, but she knew so exactly what she wanted that I did not think of protesting. I left her and went across the hall to the other room. I sat there, facing the open door, waiting for her to come in. There was nothing in my mind at all but my expectation of her appearance. When she came, she came with a sweep and a flourish, and put the coffee tray down on the table beside me. "No brandy?" I said.

Just for a moment she looked at me with surprise. "Do you want some?" she said. "Roger's got some somewhere."

I said, "Good God, no," and she smiled again and poured out the coffee. But the effervescence was gone for the moment. We drank our coffee, looking at each other but not speaking, while the tension mounted and mounted in the silence.

Presently she said, "Will you ever come back here?"

"I don't know," I said, and did not.

She said, "Better not, surely."

"Perhaps," I said. "I don't know. If I don't come here, you must come to me."

She said, "I'll do that, of course." She got up and I got up too. She went slowly toward the door.

I said, "Shall I bring the tray?"

She shook her head. "Leave the damned thing," she said. "I'll do it in the morning."

I followed her out into the hall, and when she went up the stairs, I went up after her. She went very slowly, and I was as conscious of every movement she made as if it was my own. At the top she stopped and turned, and for a moment we faced each other for the last time across the invisible dividing line. Then we simply reached out and took hold of each other. There is no mistaking the feeling when the body suddenly surrenders itself. It is the same whether or not the mind goes with it. Here I thought it did, but I was not assuming anything. I let her go and stood back from her a little, but we still held each other by one hand. Then she drew back to her side of the line, and, still holding my hand, drew me with her.

I had never seen her room before. I looked it over with a sort of breathless appraisal, while I shut the door behind me with my free hand. It was a good room, perfect for my money. There were books and pictures, elegance but no frills at all. The walls were white. The whole room smelled faintly of her, and it was warm, because she had left a fire burning when she came downstairs.

She turned and took my other hand, and stood there looking at me. All the assurance was gone. Her mouth drooped and she looked suddenly frightened. She said, "Shall I take everything off?"

"Yes, please," I said.

"Now?"

"Now," I said.

"Help me, then." She turned her back for me to undo her zipper.

I said, "Of course I'll help you. There's nothing to be frightened of."

"No?" she said. "I'm scared out of my wits."

I helped her undress, but by now I was as clumsy-handed as she was. Assurance came again only when all our clothes were off. She surrendered herself, as she did everything, quite deliberately but totally without reserve.

When I woke, there were the beginnings of daylight in the windows. Cynthia was still asleep. She lay with her back to me, and her dark hair covered all the top of her body. I looked at her for a moment, incredulous of such perfection. Then I turned and lay on my back, staring at the dark ceiling. I knew now what the capital A's meant. It was something Dick's professor had said.

Not average, Avebury. Avebury was the great henge monument that had been a religious center for a thousand years. There was something here, at Llanglas, comparable with it, but bigger. Twice as big, if I remembered Dick's note correctly. I tried to think what it would have meant to him. And to Merrion, too, surely. He might be a medievalist, but he owned the place. Anything could happen with a thing like that at stake.

I put aside the bedclothes, very gently, so as not to wake Cynthia, and started to get out of bed.

CHAPTER 14

I DROPPED my clothes in a heap on the floor of my room, still in an indeterminate bundle, as I had picked them up off the floor of Cynthia's. I was naked and shivering in the cold morning air. I took my dressing gown off the hook on the door and bundled it round me, but it was cold itself and did not do me much good. I pulled my copies of Dick's notes out of the drawer and looked at the second one again in the faint gray light. It looked quite different now. Now it meant, "Average interval perhaps 36 feet, as in the Avebury outer circle. Total probably about two hundred, as against a hundred at Avebury." I thought there was only one thing it could mean, but I did not see how it could. I put the papers back in the drawer. At any rate, there was only one thing to be done, and I could not do it here.

I shivered again. For a moment I stood there undecided, clutching my dressing gown to me. Then, as instinctively and compulsively as you stretch out a cold hand to the fire, I went back along the corridor. Cynthia was sitting up in bed with her knees drawn up. The bedclothes were clutched tight round her knees and her hair spread down between her back and the pillow. She looked as desolate as a deserted child. She looked at me, still uncertain, as I came in. "I thought you'd gone," she said.

I shook my head, and the shake spread all over my body, as it had once before when I talked to her on the dark stairs. "You're cold," she said. There was the same concern in her voice, only this time she did not order me into a hot bath. She said, "Come here." She threw back the bedclothes and opened her arms to me.

I dropped my dressing gown on the floor. "I warn you," I said, "I really am cold."

She gasped, as you gasp when you step into cold water, but the gasp turned to what was almost a giggle, so that the image of the child came momentarily back into my mind. She said, "My goodness, you are. Never mind, I'll warm you." The child vanished irretrievably. Next time it was she who woke first, and by then the sun fell full on her eastern window. She had sat up in bed and was leaning over me, so that I saw her breasts from underneath. I put my hands up to her, but she shook her head. "Go on," she said. "Go and get dressed. I'm new to this, even if you aren't." I kissed each breast once, lightly, and then went and did what I was told. When I finally came out of my room, I could smell coffee. By then I had made up my mind.

We had a curiously cheerful, businesslike breakfast. I think Cynthia had made her mind up too. The fact that our two decisions were incompatible was not fully clear to either of us. She said, "When will you be getting off?"

"After breakfast. You're very brisk about it. Aren't you going to hang on my neck and say, 'That was the nightingale and not the lark'?"

"Be practical," she said. "And be considerate. I need time to—well, recover. Have you no experience of virgins?"

"Now that I come to think of it, no, I haven't."

"Well, think of it, then." She had her hair down on

the nape of her neck again, and next to no make-up on, but she looked very sleek. "In fact," she said, "I've been very lucky. I have never had any real wish to lose my virtue before. When I did wish to, I lost it, good and proper. So many people seem to do it without meaning to, or at least in a state of wild indecision. That can't be very satisfactory."

"I know," I said. "'Now by my morning sickness, I have lost my virtue to this rude and rammish clown.' That sort of thing."

She said, "You're very Shakespearean this morning. Full of quotations. But you can forget about my morning sickness. And you weren't rude or rammish. You were very gentle. Thorough, I grant you, but gentle."

"We aim to please," I said.

"Nonsense," she said, "you aim to please yourself."

I said, "It's the same thing, or should be."

She smiled at me, suddenly and brilliantly. "Dear Mark," she said, "you really are very nice. But we don't have to decide too much straight away, do we?"

"Only when I shall next see you."

"When Roger comes back. I expect he'll be here for a bit. I can get away then. That's the understanding."

"All right," I said. "I'll wait till then as best I can. Now I'd better go out and see to the car."

"I'll give you the key," she said. She took the keys, there in front of me, out of the kitchen drawer and gave them to me.

I was on my way out to the shed when I suddenly remembered the tools in the wood.

I did not know what was going to happen at all, but I knew I could not leave them there. As soon as I was out of sight of the house, I ran. It did not take me long to get them back to the big shed. I did not have to pull out the staple, because both keys were on the same bunch. I wiped the rust off the tools as best I could and put them back where I had found them. I looked at the hexagonal nut, lying where I had put it against the wall of the shed. I hesitated, but I did not want to put it back on the bolt, not yet. I still did not know enough for that. I did not think anyone would notice it was missing. I was just leaving the shed when I remembered something. I looked round, and almost at once found the two things I was looking for. There were three long heavy timbers laid neatly one on top of the other against the far wall. I went over and looked at them. The marks of the tackle were on all of them, not far from one end. A gyn, as I had thought. The other thing I found was a pair of iron spikes, all of three feet long and hooked at the top, which would be used to anchor the winch. These too had signs of wear. The winch had been used all right. I went out and clicked the lock shut over the staple. Then I opened the smaller shed and ran my car out on to the gravel in front of the house.

When I went inside, Cynthia was nowhere to be seen. I put the keys on the kitchen table and went upstairs to pack.

When I came down with the cases, Cynthia was there. She came out to see me off. I said, "You will be all right?"

"Of course I'll be all right. Why shouldn't I be? I always am, here."

"That's perfectly true," I said. "I mustn't handicap myself, or insult you, by starting to feel protective about you. Anything less like the little woman I never saw. All the same, I should like to think you'll miss me to some extent. I shall certainly miss you."

She took both my hands in hers and shook them slightly. "Don't worry," she said. "I'll miss you, all right. I'll be wanting you long before the fortnight's up. It's odd how well I seem to know that part of myself already. And yet I've never wanted anybody before."

"Shall I write?"

"No. No, I don't think so, not at this stage. Once you

start writing, you start analyzing things. You can't help it, merely finding the words. With speech you can get by on a series of crashing clichés. I mean in moments of stress. Have you noticed? But you couldn't do it on paper. You'd have to try to make sense of it, and I don't believe in that, not yet. Let the thing develop on its own for a bit. We can make sense of it later."

"All right. When you see your way clear, just write and tell me when and where to meet you. You know where to find me."

"I'll do that. Now you'd better go."

We kissed, very seriously, as if we both knew what we meant by it. Then I got into the car and drove off. She had gone into the house before I was through the gate.

I hardly saw the village as I drove through it, and this time I was conscious of no lifting of the spirit as I went out through the gap in the hills. My double burden lay the more heavily on me the further I got from Llanglas. I headed south on the main road. I pretended I did not know where I was going, but I knew well enough. Anyway, it was high time I saw Avebury. I could not think how I had missed it all these years. But then, look at all the other national monuments I had not seen either. It is only the tourist or the expert who really sees these things. I drove on, knowing now where I was going, but not knowing what I should do when I got there, or what would come of it.

I came to Avebury in the afternoon. I came from the north, on the road from Swindon. We were back in the silent golden weather, and the downs lay in huge folds all round me as I drove. It was all very different from the country I had left. The trees stood up in tufts and neatly outlined patches, concealing nothing. Even to the inexpert eye, the scars of thousands of years of human interference lay all over the landscape. I saw simultaneously the sign saying Avebury and a bunch of petrol pumps on the side of the road. Then the road jinked in between the green shoulders of the bank, and just inside the bank, as dominant and forbidding as an armorial gateway, three huge stones stood up in the sun.

They looked enormous, far bigger than the one I had left behind at Llanglas. I think they must have been special stones, flanking the entrance in the original design, because I saw others later that were certainly no bigger than my buried stone. The bank and ditch looked bigger and steeper, too. I followed the road in, past other stones standing inside the circle of the earthwork, as the dancing man's stone, before the trees grew round it and it was chipped down and civilized, must have stood up in the middle of the huge open arena at Llanglas. I put the car obediently in the car park and walked out to explore. The hand of the Ministry of Works lay heavy but innocuous on the whole enormous sanctuary. Everything was very neat and orderly in the sunlight. There was next to no one about.

Part of the village, including the pub, had been built inside the circle. The church, which must have been there longer than most of it, stood just outside. It stood there, stubborn and disapproving, on what must have been the very edge of the great bank, brooding over the whole abomination but safely out of harm's way. I wondered if the men who had built it had heard what had happened at Llanglas. Somebody must have, even if the outrage had been kept out of the chronicles. They had even labored to level the great earthwork at this point, so that some of the faithful were buried in the once enormously sacred and now execrable soil. It seemed a mean thing to do, to post your dead as garrison in land you were too holy or too scared to occupy yourself, but I do not expect the early Christians of these parts saw it like that. I left the road and went up over the well-trimmed turf to the western side of the bank.

There was a whole line of stones here, standing at

regular intervals along the curving inner edge of the ditch. They were natural stones, not dressed at all. They had been brought here and up-ended in their chalk sockets with a sort of monstrous ingenuity and what must have been prodigious and highly organized labor. In between, where the gaps were too wide for regularity, small concrete pylons marked what were obviously the sites of the missing stones. As I had thought, the bank and ditch were enormous. They must have been twice the height of the Llanglas circle, but on plan the circle was very much smaller. In that dark and tangled woodland it had been very difficult to get any idea of distance over the ground, but I knew how long it had taken me to walk round it. Even allowing for the clearer going, it would not take me half the time here. I walked on round the circle, not bothering to time myself, but trying to get the whole picture clear in my mind.

I crossed the tarmac where the road ran out through the southern entrance, and when I came up on to the bank on the far side, there were no stones at all. There was a bunch of stones standing on my left hand, well inside the circle of the ditch, but on the edge of the ditch itself there were none. They must have been there once. The regularity and completeness of the original design made anything else impossible. But they were not there now. Or not visibly there. I stopped short and let myself consider this. Dick, probing his way with the iron spike round the circle of Llanglas, seemed to have counted stones and even calculated the distance between them; and there not a stone was standing. Whatever had happened there could have happened here. But this was all nonsense. Avebury was not a lost site like Llanglas. It had surely all been investigated and worked out long ago. Someone would know. I had only to ask. I walked on, still with no clear intention in my head, but determined to complete the circle.

When I got back to the western side of the bank,

where the stones were, I took half a dozen of them and paced out the distances between them. I do not guarantee the length or regularity of my stride, but it was twelve yards, more or less, from stone to stone. As Dick's note had said, thirty-six feet. A hundred stones, thirty-six feet apart. And at Llanglas, if he was right, as many as two hundred, set at the same intervals by whatever primeval module the designers had used in the setting out. And all buried, all safe under the turf, all cast away, as the church ordained, where they could not be found by their worshippers. Now they had been found, centuries later, by the eager and informed curiosity of the expert, on to their hiding place like a terrier on a rat-hole. In terms of present-day interest, it was an enormous secret. Dick had known it. Merrion knew it. Now I knew it. I sat down on the turf, just clear of the line of stones, and tried to think what I ought to do.

I did not hear him coming over the soft turf, but he said, "Good afternoon," and I looked up to find him standing almost over me. The benign, educated face went with the voice. He was an elderly, tweedy man and very gentlemanly. I said, "Good afternoon," and started to get up.

"Don't get up," he said. "I was going to sit down myself, as a matter of fact. My wife will be along with the car in a minute or two. May I join you?"

I said, "Please do," and he sat down, with the calculated, slightly laborious movements of his age, but with no loss of dignity. He looked as if he had sat down on the turf when he felt like it all his life and was not going to give it up now. He ran a mild, slightly quizzical eye over me, as if he was making up his mind what I was doing there.

He said, "Interested in this sort of thing?"

"Interested but ignorant."

This pleased him. "Yes," he said, "yes, that's what I

thought. I saw you, I think, pacing the distances between the stones just now. It's all in the books, of course."

"It must be," I said. "Can you tell me one thing? Where are all the missing stones? What happened to them?"

"They may not be missing," he said. "Not altogether. They may be buried. Most of the stones in this sector were buried until Alexander Keiller dug them up and put them back in their original holes. Some, unfortunately, have gone altogether. We know they were there, but they have been destroyed."

"Hence the concrete pylons?" I said. "But who did all this, and when?"

"They buried them," he said, "in the Middle Ages. It was the right thing to do. The stones were anathema, of course, the work of devils and no doubt stumbling blocks to the less than faithful. Incidentally, it also cleared the land for cultivation, so you got the best of both worlds. But mainly it was the Church's doing, I think."

"But they didn't break them up," I said, "merely buried them?"

"They probably didn't know how to, or they might have. They didn't find that out until the eighteenth century, thank goodness. Then they broke up a lot. But you see, the odd thing is that by then they had forgotten how many stones were buried. Or at least they didn't know where most of them were. So the stones were spared. The barbarism of the Age of Faith frustrated the materialism of the Age of Reason. A nice touch of irony. I have often wondered what the medieval zealots would have thought if they had known they were saving the stones for posterity. It must have been hard work, too. Even dangerous. There was the strange case of the barber-surgeon."

A car came in from the southwest, hooting as it came,

and he struggled to his feet. "There she is," he said. "I must be off. Mustn't keep her waiting. Nice to have met you."

I was on my feet too. "What happened to the barber-surgeon?" I said.

He was already on the move. "Oh," he said, "he got caught, and serve him right. Mustn't stop now. It's all in the museum. Go and have a look round. You'll see it all there." He waved a hand and was off. He was still a good mover, but he moved as if the devil was after him.

CHAPTER 15

I FOLLOWED HIM slowly along the edge of the ditch, back toward the road and the car park. I saw him scramble guiltily into the waiting car, and the car move off with a jerk that must have taken millimeters off the clutch plates. I wondered if I should ever run like that. At least I did not believe Cynthia would ever do that to a clutch. But mainly I wondered about the barber-surgeon. From what the mild man had said, he had been one of the medieval stone-buriers. Perhaps, as a man of professional status, the leader of a demolition squad. But he had been caught, and serve him right, the mild man had said. There was something suddenly chilling about it that I did not like the sound of. Anyway, it was all in the museum. I moved off, unhappily but compulsively, toward it.

The signposts pointed me through the lychgate and across the churchyard. On my right, between the graves, I could just see the broad ripple in the turf which marked the line of the leveled bank. I went round the west end of the church, hardly looking at it. Anywhere else I should have thought it a nice little country church. Here I resented it. I remembered suddenly Merrion's expression as he looked at the desolation of the ruined abbey. I understood a little of what I thought he felt.

Already, if I had to take sides, I was no longer on the side of the angels.

I pushed open the door of the museum and went in. It was completely quiet, and had the faintly preservative smell of such places. A man in uniform behind a sort of counter took my money and went back to his evening paper. I turned left and went slowly along the showcases.

This was very much Dick's world. Or one of his worlds, perhaps, the one I had tended to forget because he had not pushed it at me. There was nothing amateurish in it at all. It was, if you like, popularized, or at any rate consciously educational. The experts were doing their best to involve the layman in their own vision, but it was an austere vision, and they did not make many concessions. With me at least they succeeded. I got involved, almost in spite of myself. I went round slowly, reading the cards, looking at the bones and the potsherds and the flint tools, trying almost feverishly to think myself back across that astonishing gap of time to the men, in all respects as human and intelligent as I was, who had done all this for the sake of something they believed in. It took me quite a while, and the afternoon light was starting to go when I came to the showcase which had been on my right when I came in at the door. It was all about the buried stones and the business of raising them, but the thing I saw first was the photograph. There was a great stone, unearthed, but lying as it was found in its burial pit, and beneath it, crushed down into the earth but just showing under the bottom edge of the stone, there was a despairing human face.

It was not a face, of course, only the remains of one, but the mouth of the skull was slightly agape, as if the man had screamed when the stone came down on top of him. It was the barber-surgeon all right. They had dug him out now, five or six hundred years too late, and stood the stone up again in its proper place. His contemporaries, brought up short in the height of their unintelligible excitement, had not done as much. They had earthed him in, hastily, where he was, with the stone on top of him and the tools of his trade still at his side, and gone home crossing themselves. I wondered if any of them had tried burying any more stones after that. But it was only the barber-surgeon who had been caught. Serve him right, perhaps, as the mild man had said. For myself I was no longer much concerned with him.

I stood there, staring at the horror, for what must have been quite a time, because after a bit I heard the man in uniform rustling his newspaper and knew he was looking at me. I expect it was closing time, and he wanted to lock up and go home to his tea. I turned and went out, not looking at him. I thought I knew now where Dick might be, and I did not want to talk about it. I walked back across the churchyard to the car park. I backed the car and got her out. Then I drove through the great circle to the south entrance, and headed south for the main road to London.

Even if it was true, it could have been an accident, obviously. It looked as if it had been an accident at Avebury six centuries earlier. The stone could have slipped when no one was ready for it. At Avebury they were trying to get the stone down, and at Llanglas they would have been trying to get it up, but I did not see that made much difference. If it was not an accident, I could think of two good reasons why Merrion might have wanted Dick out of the way. The odd thing is that I did not mind very much whether it had been an accident or not. What I could not bear, if the thing was true, was Dick's being left there. I knew why he would have been left there, even if it had been an accident. That was the one thing I did know. He would have been left there because, however the thing had happened, there could be no explanation that did not involve the stone, and the stone, all the stones, the whole damned place, was Merrion's secret. It meant that Merrion was mad, of course, or getting on that way. He could be, too. He was not a prehistorian, he was a medievalist. He would not have seen the thing as Dick saw it. It was vaster and older and more important than anything he had ever set his mind to, and it was there, on his private property, and he was not even qualified to deal with it. Alive or dead, Dick would have taken the secret out of his hands, and when it came to the point, he might not have been able to bear it. And now I had the secret too, as Dick had had it, and I could not bear to leave things as they were. That was a second thing I was certain of. I had very little idea what would happen if I did not leave things as they were, but I knew I could not. I had to know. I got to London late and a little dazed, and let myself into my cold flat.

I got the place warmed up and made myself a meal of some sort, because I knew I needed it, but there was no comfort anywhere. I did not let myself think of Cynthia at all. The nightmare lay between me and her, and I did not know, if I once dispelled it, whether she would still be there. I already knew what I had to do. The plan of action pieced itself together in my mind because the action had to be taken, but I did not know what the end of it would be. I even went round the place sorting out the things I should need and making a mental list of what I should have to get. After a bit there was nothing more I could do, and I went to bed. I slept, too, not at once, but before very long. I was tired out physically, and I had made up my mind. It is indecision that keeps you awake, not ignorance or despair, and I was conscious of no indecision at all. The next day I finished what I had to do and put the things I needed in the car. I left London early in the afternoon and headed northwest.

It was a relief to be driving again, and driving toward a specific objective. It was a relief to be committed to a course of action which involved practical problems but as far as I could see no imponderables. I knew exactly what I had to do. I knew what I had to do it with and where everything was. I knew, to a day or two, how long I had for the job. I was not certain I could do it, but I thought I could, and I knew where the difficulties lay. I could, and did, put everything else out of my mind. I drove fast, partly because from now on I was in fact working against the clock, but mainly because I took refuge, deliberately, in urgency.

In fact I overdid it, because I came out on to the main road south of the Llanglas turning before it was fully dark, and I had to stop and wait for the light to go. I did not like this, I did not want to stop doing anything, but it was indispensable. This, as I saw it, was the one really risky part of the whole job, and I did not want to do anything to increase the odds against me. It was fully dark when I turned in through the village, but still early in the evening. This was a good time, because everyone had just got in and shut their doors and drawn their curtains. Later some of them would come out again, but for the moment they had had enough of the world outside. I do not think anyone took any notice of me, even if anyone saw me. I drove nearly as far as the gate. Then I stopped and unloaded the car. There was quite a lot of stuff, but it was packed for carrying. I dumped it all behind a rock on the hillside, ten yards or so up from the road, where the lights of a car could not pick it up. But I did not think there would be a car. When it was all stowed, I backed the car, very cautiously, in the width of the road and drove back the way I had come.

I had not settled the details of this next bit, but I knew what I had to do. When I got back to the main road, I turned left and headed north. I wanted a place where I could garage my car and get a taxi, but not from the same people. A small town would be best, but a biggish village might do. It involved making sure of the taxi first, and then seeing if there was anywhere else I could put the car in. I found it at the second attempt. I put the car in for a week and took the taxi back to Llanglas village. It was all quite expensive, but I had thought of that and brought plenty of cash. I paid off the taxi on the outskirts of the village. From there on I walked. I did not walk through the village, because these days a man walking is much more conspicuous than a car, even if he does not have to carry an illuminated number plate. I expect that will come, when they start taxing pedestrians instead of cars. I worked my way round the village through the fields and picked up the side road not far east of the gap in the hills. After that I stuck to the road. If a car had come either way, I should have had plenty of time to get out of the lights, but none did.

I took my clothes first, because if they were found, they would be identifiable. If this was an unnecessary refinement, it was the sort of way I was thinking. I went for the practical details like a drug, because they kept my mind off the implications. There was not much in the way of clothes, obviously, but such as they were, I took them first. I took some of the camping gear with them. I thought I could do the rest in one trip. I did not intend the first stage to be a long one. I had had a good deal of experience of this sort of thing, and did it all, quite deliberately, as well as I knew how. When I had got the first load complete and comfortable, I walked along what was left of the road and in at the gate.

I had driven out of the gate less than thirty-six hours before. It felt a long time ago, and seemed to have very little connection with anything I was doing now. I saw the lights on in the house behind drawn curtains, but it felt like a strange house, and I did not know what was going on inside. I went left, going softly over the gravel, went round the end of the sheds and took the track into the wood. I knew the place so well by now that I saw my blaze on the tree without using my torch. I had never tried to find it at night before, but it showed almost startlingly white in the darkness. I turned off into the wood and put my load down where I had put the tools. It was just as I was going back that I remembered turning out of the bushes and finding old Evans coming along the track. I checked and went cautiously. If there was anyone on the track at this time of night, it would be him, though I thought it was too early for him.

There was no one there. I went as quickly as I could after that, but always peering ahead in the darkness, watching for the tall fantastic shape coming toward me. Once I had got back to the stuff and loaded myself a second time, I did not have this to worry about. There was no one on the tarmac. There was no daylight left at all, but it was a clear night, and you could see quite a distance on the glimmer of the road. Even if he was coming, he was some way behind me and I could keep ahead of him. But I did not think he was.

I got all the rest of the gear on to me in the second load. It was very heavy, but I did not mean to take all of it beyond the blaze on the tree. My base camp, I called it—I was still making as much as possible of the whole maneuver. When I got there, I off-loaded the tent, which was heavy. It was too heavy, really, for this sort of thing, but it was the only one I had, and it would be comfortable and convenient when I had it up. I could even do my cooking inside it, at least at night. Then I went straight on with the rest of the second load. I had still no intention of going any way but along the top of the bank. I thought I could probably move along it without a light, and if I got into the middle of the wood in the darkness, God knows where I should find myself. When I came to the gap, I turned and went straight up. I had been right. It was not half the height of the Avebury bank. All the same, it was a prodigious work. I had all the constructional details now. Antler picks, they had had, and blade-bone shovels, and baskets to carry the loose earth. There must have been an enormous labor force here four thousand years ago, organized to the last inch, and driven on by the same tremendous communal urge as had raised the early cathedrals in the country's next great religious ferment. And we still, most of us, thought of the Stone Age as men with apelike jaws crouching in caves and grunting at each other.

My eyes were working well now, and I made surprisingly good speed. This was desirable, because I was timing myself, to make sure I should not overshoot the mark in the darkness. I was going slower, obviously, than I had before, but not all that slower. When I had been going nearly long enough, I got the torch out and flashed it occasionally on the far side of the ditch. In fact I need not have worried. I knew the place well enough, and crossed the ditch before I got there. I stopped before I came to the disturbed soil. I did not want to walk over the stone, not now. I put my load down on the edge of the ditch and straightened my shoulders. I was tired, of course, but still moving well within myself. I wanted to be tired, anyway, before I was done. It was all a part of what I was doing.

I started back at once. There was no question of timing now. I would just keep on until I had finished. I went cautiously along the length of track between the bank and my base camp, but once I was moving back toward the bank again, I felt secure. I left the tent, but took the whole of my original first load. It was heavier than the stuff I had carried along the bank the first time and I was getting tired now. I must have gone a good deal slower, but time had ceased to count, and I did not have to worry about finding the place, not with all the first lot of stuff stacked on the far side of the ditch. I was faintly surprised when I came to it. I put my load down with it. When I had it off, I found that one of my shoulders was slightly sore. This would not do, because I had a lot of carrying to do during the next few days. I thought I could pad it for carrying the tent. In any case, the tent by itself was very little compared with what I had been carrying.

When I got back to the blaze the second time, I did not turn into the wood to where the tent was. I went straight on until I came to the back of the house. I had not meant to do this at all. I turned left and walked round the back to the north side. The kitchen window would have been uncurtained, but there was no light in it. There was a light in the window above, but the curtains were drawn. It must be later than I thought. I stared at it for a moment, but I was too tired to feel anything much. I turned and went back for the tent.

Once I was back on the bank again, there was nothing more to think about anyhow. Apart from the track between the house and the dancing man's stone, the wood was all my own, and would be for another week at least. All the same, I pitched the tent among the bushes in the bottom of the ditch, almost next to the winch. I had to do a little clearance of the ground before I got it up, but I thought the result would be satisfactory, even by daylight. I moved all my gear into the tent, which had room for it. Then I went out along the bank, for the last time, to fill my water can at the stream, but this was not very far to go.

I had food ready to eat. I had not expected to want to get a meal ready tonight, and I did not. I ate what I had ready and drank quite a lot of the water. Then I got my clothes off, rubbed myself down a bit and crawled into my sleeping bag. Once I stopped moving, there was not a sound anywhere. The wood was completely still. I was no longer afraid of it. I thought I should be afraid of the abbey if I got into it in the dark, but here there was nothing to frighten me. It was not I who had pulled the stones down, but the monks, and they had long since paid for it. I lay quite still and almost empty-minded, and after a time I slept.

CHAPTER 16

Some time toward morning I was awakened by the rustling of the fallen leaves on top of the bank. It seemed to go on for quite a time, and I drifted gradually awake listening to it. I thought the wind must have got up, but when I was fully awake, I could hear no sound from the trees, and there was no movement in the tent. By that time the noise of the leaves had stopped too. I went to sleep again, and the next time I woke there was daylight showing through the tent. I stretched and found I was a bit stiff, but no worse. After a little I got up and made tea and cooked myself a proper meal. Then I went out to see what I had to do.

There was only one thing I had to do that day. I had to get the winch in position on the edge of the ditch. I could not start to get the rest of the gear from the shed until well after dark. In any case, if I could not get the winch up, the thing was hopeless from the start. I thought that originally two men had got it up, and that later one man had maneuvered it to the edge and rolled it down the slope. If that was so, it meant that it was possible to shift it singlehanded on the flat. Merrion might well be one of those people who are a lot stronger than they look. He looked soft and a bit out of condition, but the muscle might be there, and the weight certainly was, which would help with a job like this. All the same, I thought I was as strong as he was. I walked all round the winch, considering it.

There was only one possible way of shifting it. This was to get it standing up on its wooden base and then move it by swinging it forward, first round one corner and then round the other. It would be an agonizingly slow business, but I thought it could be done. The slope of the ditch would make two kinds of difficulty. The first was the obvious one that I should be moving it against gravity. The second was the danger that at more than a certain angle it might become top-heavy and tend to turn over and roll down again. The first I could mitigate to some extent by not trying to go straight up the slope, but taking it at a bit of a slant. This would mean that when I got it to the top, it would be some way from where I wanted it, but at least the difference could be made up on the flat. The second I must guard against as best I could when I came up against it. In fact the greatest single difficulty I met was getting it up on its base, because this meant taking a lot of the dead weight of the ironmongery.

I found I could just about lift the top of it off the ground, but there was no question of getting it in one go to the point where its center of gravity would go past the vertical and bring the whole thing over on to its base. There was nothing for it but to lift it a little at a time and underpin it with some sort of crib as I went. I cleared the bushes from round it and then went into the wood looking for suitable bits of timber. In the end I found a selection of logs I thought would do, but it took me an exasperatingly long time. I think it was then that the time factor really began to worry me. If Cynthia had got it right, I had four clear days before Merrion came back, and I knew from this point onward that I was going to need all of it. After a bit, time became an obsession with me, and drove me on well past the point of normal exhaustion. For the moment I worked with a sort of steady desperation on the winch.

As with all such jobs, I acquired a technique as I went on, lifting the dead weight six inches or so and then pushing the next piece of timber under it, first with my feet and then, as it got higher, with my knees. When I broke off for a rest and food, I had got to a point where I could crouch and use my own weight against the weight of the metal. When I came back to it, it looked a good deal better than I expected, and it was not long afterward that I suddenly felt it very nearly in balance. I was seized with the fear that when it went, its weight might carry it too far and it might fall over on its other side. The only thing to do was to make the last lift from the front, pulling instead of pushing, so that I should be there to steady it if it looked like doing that. I tried this once, but it would not come past the point of balance, and I had to let it settle back on its timbers again. I went round, heaved and added one more bit of wood to the crib. Then I went round to the front again and pulled, and this time it came. I do not think in fact it would have turned itself over the other way, but I had my weight against it in case. The crazy crib of logs collapsed as the weight came off it, but the winch stood up firm and secure on its wooden base. The first battle was over. It was now well into the afternoon.

I gave myself half an hour's rest, timed by my watch. Then I started the long haul up the slope of the ditch. It turned out to be easier than I had dared to hope, but it was desperately slow. I was thankful I had not got the height and slope of the Avebury ditch to contend with. Time blurred a bit after that. I went on swinging the monstrous contraption first one way and then the other, but at least it was solidly based and showed no tendency to topple over. I was nearly up to the top when I noticed that it was starting to get dark, but by then I was too tired to let time worry me. I had the winch standing on the flat top before I went down to the tent to rest and get my supper. It was still several yards from where it had to be, but my mind was easy. There was nothing left now, in the whole damned maneuver, that could turn out to be physically impossible. There was the long labor of bringing up the gear from the shed, and there was the applied skill of rigging the tackle when I had it on the spot. But the problem was under control. It was only a question of time now.

I cooked and ate my supper outside the tent in the dusk. There was a very slight breeze moving in the tops of the trees now, but down here the air hardly moved, and it was still mercifully mild. When I had finished and cleared up, I went straight up and maneuvered the winch into its working position. It settled exactly into the impression it had made before and only needed anchoring. It was fully dark now, but not late enough to risk a first journey to the shed. In any case, I could not go on, even walking and carrying, without a proper rest. I went down to the tent, took off my shoes and top clothes and crawled into the sleeping bag. The one thing I could not risk was getting cold. I went to sleep almost at once, the blank, bottomless sleep of physical exhaustion and a full belly. But I knew I could not let myself sleep too long. Over the next stage the nights were going to be more precious than the days. Some time after midnight my subconscious kicked me awake. I was warm, and the food and sleep had done me good. I felt in fair shape, at least for the sort of prolonged but relatively mild effort I had to make. I got dressed, put my torch in my pocket and crawled out into the darkness. It was still mild and dry. There was no moon.

I thought that in the morning, when I might have time on my hands, I must try to find a direct way through the wood from the end of the track. There must be one. I did not for a moment believe that Merrion came all the way round the earthwork to get here. But it was a job for daylight. For the moment the only thing was to follow the route I knew. I went up on to the bank, turned right and began my walk round to the track.

I did not worry, either during that night or during any of the nights that followed, about running into old Evans. There was no logical reason for this. I think the truth is that he was a risk I simply had to take. I had to carry a great deal of stuff along the track from the shed to the earthwork, and time was the enemy now. Once I was away from the shed, concealment, or even caution, was simply not practicable, apart from the fact that I worked all the time in full darkness. It occurred to me afterward that it might very likely need a moon to bring the old lunatic out, but I did not argue it this way at the time. I simply went ahead because there was nothing else I could do.

It was only just before I got to the shed that it occurred to me to worry about the nut on the staple. It was only a faint worry, even then, but I was glad I had not thought of it before. If someone had put the nut back, it would have made nonsense of everything I had done so far. But it was only Cynthia who could have, and I could see no possible reason to suppose she had. In fact when I got my hand on the staple, I knew at once that it was still free. Even so, the bolt took more getting out than I had expected, but it came eventually. I swung the hasp open with the staple still locked through it, opened one door and went into the shed, shutting the door behind me. It was only then that I allowed myself to use the torch.

On this too I had done a good deal of rather feverish mental organization. I could move the stuff only at night. The object, if it could be managed, was to get enough gear to the site each night to give me something to work on during the following day, or as much of the day as I found it possible to work. The spade was the first and obvious thing to take. After that I planned to take the components of the gyn and the block and tackle that went immediately with them. Getting them up and rigged would give me all of a day's work. But the timber legs were very long and heavy. Each one meant a separate journey, and not an easy one at that. I could of course use the anchor hooks for the winch and the maul to drive them at any time now, but the job would take no time at all to do, and to take them at this stage would be a mistake.

Even here in the shed I was conscious of the pressure of time and wasted no more than I could help. I put the spade outside the shed and went back and looked over the tackle. I picked out the biggest block, which I had no doubt had been used on the gyn, and a length of rope which would serve to lash the timbers together at the apex and hang the block under them. Even with the spade this meant a fairly light load, but it was an awkward one to handle, and in any case there was no chance of taking one of the legs, which were the next item on my list. I took the stuff out, shut the shed and put the staple and hasp back into position, but with the bolt pushed no more than half home. I should be back before long, and it was pitch-dark anyway. The most superficial appearance of normality would do. I set out again for the earthwork, making all the speed I could. I carried the rope coiled on my shoulder and the block and spade in my hands. My idea was to come back for the first of the timber legs and get it to the site that night. Then during the day I could do the digging round the stone and if possible find a more direct way through the wood. The next night I could bring up the two remaining legs, and I should then be able to work on the gyn the following day. It was all very nicely calculated. What I had not foreseen was the appalling labor of carrying a timber of this size along the top of the bank in the dark. It was only when I got back to the shed the second time and tried lifting the first of the legs that I had some idea what I was up against.

I put the torch, switched on, against one wall and left the door open. I did not like doing this, but I had to have light to maneuver the unwieldy load out of the shed. I got my shoulder under the timber and got it balanced. Its dead weight shocked me a bit, but I got it out through the door without knocking anything over or breaking the window. I up-ended it against the side of the shed. Then I went in and collected the torch and shut the door. This time I pushed the bolt of the staple right home. I knew already that I should not be back that night. I dropped the torch in my pocket, shouldered the timber and started out along the track.

It was not a matter of intense and violent effort, as moving the winch had been, but as a sheer endurance test the winch had nothing on it. I had padded both shoulders thickly with a sweater, but even so the sharp edges of the timber bit painfully into the muscles, especially at the side of the neck. When I rested, I merely put one end of the leg on the ground, brought it up to a near vertical and leant against it. I was not going to risk having to lift the whole damned thing off the ground again. Later it occurred to me to lean it against a suitable tree, so that I was free to work my arms loose and sit down if I wanted to. I do not know how many times I rested before I even got to the earthwork. It was far more often than I had expected.

So far it had been open track and relatively easy going underfoot. It was when I got up on to the bank that I really came up against it. The trees did not grow thickly on the bank, but there were trees there, and I had to find my way between them. With a heavy load projecting six feet or so in front of me, and the night as dark as pitch, this was a nightmare. As I got weaker, my own balance on my feet and the balance of the timber on my shoulder got more precarious, so that a head-on collision would have had the timber on the ground and maybe me as well. I did not in fact drop it until I was getting well round toward the site. When I did, I did not think I had it in me to pick it up again. I sat down on it where it lay and let my head hang forward over my knees. I was getting very near the end of my strength. The fact that I was due to repeat the whole performance twice the next night did nothing to comfort me. The only hope was that before then I might find a shorter and perhaps easier line through the wood.

I sat there, crouched over that damned piece of wood, until I had to do something or get really cold. I thought I would leave it where it was and walk on to see how much further there was to go. Walking without any load on my shoulder was in fact the best thing I could have done. It loosened me up and let the strained muscles get back into a more normal way of working. I came to the site before I dared to hope for it. There was not more than a hundred yards to go, perhaps less. It was now or never. I went straight back, put the timber up on my shoulder with less difficulty than I had expected and got moving again. I felt immensely better now that the end was a calculated and feasible distance away. Physically I was as near exhaustion as ever, but mentally I was on top of the job again. I rested only once more before I put the leg down as near as possible where I thought it would have to go. I remember, as a final gesture of bravado, putting it down quite gently on the earth, when it would have done it no harm simply to get from under it and let it fall.

I went down to the tent, brewed myself a pot of tea and ate some biscuits with it. It was getting on for half-past three. When I finally got into my sleeping bag, I did not expect to sleep at once, and did not. I dozed off gradually as my nerves and muscles unwound themselves. When I heard the rustle of the leaves on the bank, I was too sleepy to take much notice of it. I woke in broad daylight with two very stiff shoulders.

CHAPTER 17

When I was ready to start, I took the spade and cleared the earth from the whole face of the stone and from all round it. It was shovel work, really, because the earth was already loose. Enough earth must have been taken out before to let the stone be lifted. There was no need for me to move anything that had not already been moved. The edge of the pit was about a foot clear of the extreme dimensions of the stone on each side. I went down, still in loose earth, until the spade went under the bottom of the stone all round. The depth of the stone, as it lay, was a good deal less than the width of the upper face. It was a sort of massive slab, not worked at all, but naturally rectangular. Originally it might have had quite sharp corners, but they had been weathered down. Merrion had said that the local rock broke away in this sort of shape. The builders could have dragged or rolled their stones down from the hills, with a good deal of gravity to help them. It would have been less of a labor than at Avebury, where they had had to collect their sarsens from the Marlborough downs and bring them in over the flat undulations of the chalk. I thought perhaps it was the plentifulness and accessibility of the stones that accounted for the huge scale of the work. Even so, it would be a stupendous work on any count.

I thought I could see the marks on the sides of the stone where the wire ropes had been taken round it for the lift. They were near the end away from the winch. The ropes would have been worked under the stone from that end. The stone could not have been lifted clear, but must have been swung up on the end nearer the winch, where it was tapered slightly to something like a point. That may have been the way it originally stood before the monks had toppled it over. I was not concerned with that. All I wanted was to repeat the lifting operation as it had been done before, and get the stone clear of the bottom of the pit.

I heaped the earth I took out well clear of the edge of the pit, leaving clear spaces at the sides where I should have to bring the gyn and tackle in. When I had done that, there was not much more I could do. Even that took me what was left of the morning and a good bit of the afternoon. With the night's work I had in prospect, it was more than enough. All the same, I got a sort of savage satisfaction from the way my muscles stood up to it. I was getting into condition fast. I had no doubt now that I could do what I had set myself to do. Time was all I wanted. I had a rest and some food. Then I set out to find a path through the wood.

I assumed, as I had thought all along, that I was pretty well on the extreme western point of the circle. This seemed likely, not only from my timing when I had originally walked round, but also because I thought Merrion would have deliberately chosen the point farthest away from the point of access. If the track ran straight in from the eastern entrance to near the center, it meant that to join the end of it from here I had to go in eastward on the radius of the circle. I fixed my line as best I could from what I could see of the curve through the trees. Then I went straight up the inner side of the ditch and into the wood.

I worked on a sense of direction only, because there was nothing else to work on. In fact the line was clearer than I had hoped and the going firm underfoot. I had not been going long when I saw the wheel marks on a patch of clear ground. They looked like a pair of rubber tyres, mounted fairly close together. It had not occurred to me before to wonder how Merrion, even with Dick to help him, had got the winch to the site. Now I knew, or at least I had a pretty good idea. They had used some sort of trolley or trailer. There was nothing like it in the shed, but it might be in one of the other buildings. I thought they could have manhandled it over the level ground between them, but Merrion could never have managed it alone. When he found himself alone, he would have rolled the winch down the far slope of the bank, hidden it as best he could and brought the trolley back empty. It all added up. It added up much too well. But at least I was on the right line.

The next thing I saw was the familiar line of tumbled masonry, half hidden among the trees on my right. I was into the abbey ruins. Presently the trees cleared ahead, and I came out into the long clearing I had looked at from the far end when Merrion had been with me. I knew where I was now. The abbey church, he said it had been. The track came close to it at the other end. I had my line, all right. It was much shorter and almost certainly easier going than the long trek round the bank. The only difficulty would be holding the line in the dark between the abbey ruins and the far side of the circle, but I thought I could mark that well enough in what was left of the daylight.

I went on, keeping to the trees just off the edge of the clearing. I did not want to go into the clearing itself. I suppose it was partly that I did not want to go where I could be seen, if there was anyone to see me. But mainly I think it was the sheer repugnance I felt to the place itself. I had felt it when Merrion had brought me there, and I felt it now, stronger than ever. I knew, of course, because Merrion had told me, that something terrible had happened here. The rest could have been my imagination. I only know that the place horrified me. Whatever the great stone circle had meant in its day, it was innocence compared with this. Only the compulsion that drove me could have brought me back here after dark, but I knew it would bring me. All the same, I kept to the edge of the trees.

I found the end of the track easily enough. I did not stay there. I turned and went back the way I had come, skirting the edge of that damned clearing as I had before. As soon as I got to the far end of it, I took out my knife and began to cut blazes on the trees. It would have taken no time at all with an axe, but my camping gear did not include one. I am not the sort of camper to cook over wood fires for the hell of it. With the knife it was slow work.

There was no need here to cut the blazes where no one else would notice them. No one would come this way while my need for secrecy lasted. I cut them at eye level and as thick as time allowed. I might have to use the torch, at least the first time, to pick them up, but that too did not matter here. I blazed my trail patiently, tree by tree, while the light went out of the wood. I saw the line of the bank ahead of me in the last of the dusk, with the piled earth showing up dark against it. There was still nothing wrong with my line. The wind was getting up now, and when I got into the tent, the wood was threshing and roaring all round me. I switched on a light and got myself a meal in the glimmering chaos. Then I crawled into my bag, gave myself three hours on the face of my watch and settled down to sleep.

I woke up when I had told myself to and lay for a little listening to the wind. There was no harm in it, so far as I was concerned, unless it made trouble with the shed doors while I was getting out the two remaining legs of the gyn. I thought they could probably be hooked back somehow. In any case, the thing to do was to get both the timbers out while I was about it and leave one in the wood close to the track while I carried the other one to the site. Opening the shed was the most vulnerable part of the job, because it meant showing a light too close to the house. The less often I did it, the better.

I got dressed and put a new battery in the torch, in case I had to use it a lot coming back through the wood. Also, I put a string loop on it, so that I could hang it on me if I wanted to. I needed both hands, God knows, to keep the timber balanced on my shoulder, and I thought that even an undirected and wavering beam ahead of me would pick up the blazes all right.

There was much less wind, when I went out into it, than I had thought there was while I was still inside the tent. It was rather like getting a boat off her moorings. The wind that feels like half a gale flapping the loose sails about turns out to be no more than a fair sailing breeze once the sails are sheeted in and the boat is under way. There was a lot of noise in the trees, of course, but that was an advantage, if anything. I still did not really believe that there would be anybody about in the wood at this time of night, but it was in any case impossible to go quietly once I had a load up. I had gone some way along the bank before I realized that I was on the bank and not on my new line through the wood. This may have been mere habit, but I think in fact I was not going through the wood until I consciously made myself do it. At any rate, there was no point in turning back now. I was not going to lose much time so long as I was walking light.

I got the two remaining legs of the gyn out of the shed without mishap. I carried the first one a few yards along the track and dumped it in the bushes. The second one I propped up against the side of the shed while I went back to look at the rest of the stuff. There was the wire rope, another couple of blocks and the spikes to anchor the winch. I should also want the maul to drive the spikes. There was another thing, too, I thought I saw a use for. It was a heavy baulk of timber, stouter than the legs of the gyn, but a good deal shorter. It was leaning against the wall at the far end of the shed, and even in the torchlight I could see that one end at least had had the corners knocked off it. I thought it had been used at some stage to prop the stone after it had been lifted. It had occurred to me that something of the sort might be needed, and there was nothing lying about in the wood that was nearly up to the job. All in all, there was at least another night's carrying there. Bar accidents, I could still just do it in time, but only just. I went out, shut the door and pushed the bolt of the staple right home. Even allowing for the shorter line through the wood, I still had enough on my hands for that night. I shouldered the timber I had left leaning against the shed and set out along the track.

I made better going than I had with the same load the night before. All the way through those four interminable nights and days I was coming to terms with my self-appointed nightmare. The more I drove myself, the tougher and cleverer I got at the job in hand, and the less I thought about anything but getting it finished in time. It was the mindless labor that carried me on, past the entrance of the earthwork, toward the middle of the pitch-black wood, where I could hardly bring myself to walk in daylight. When I came to the standing stone, I leant the timber against a tree on the other side of the track and went deliberately across to it and touched it. It seemed warm under my hand. Then I took out my torch and shone it flat across the far face of the stone. I was not afraid of the dancing man now. I thought I was on his side and he on mine, but I could not have said why. The torchlight threw him up in all his monstrous vivacity, and for a second or two I looked at him, capering in his pool of white light while the dark wood roared round the pair of us. It was the last time I saw him. I switched out the torch and put it away and went back to my timber on the far side of the track. Then I shouldered it and went on into the desolation the dancing man had created and still watched over.

I think on a still night it would have been worse. Whatever it was that cried from the ground, it could not quite make itself heard in the tumult. Only nothing could have made me stop there, however desperately I needed to put my load down. I went on along the edge of the trees, with the glimmering emptiness on my left and the black roaring trees on my right, driving myself and my piece of wood out of reach of the horror that hung about there. When I got to the far end of the clearing, I went on a dozen paces into the wood and let the leading end of the timber down on to the ground. I upended it until the weight came off my shoulders, and then I clutched it and leant against it for a minute or two, hanging my head and feeling the ache die out of my muscles while the sweat ran into my eyes. Then I got the torch out and shone it into the wood ahead. Ahead of me there was nothing, but when I swung the beam, it picked up a blaze on a tree a little way to my left. I was not much off the line. I left the torch on and hung it on its string round my neck. I could still just see the blaze. I got the timber up on to my shoulder again and moved over toward it. I picked up another before I got to the first, and after that there was no trouble. The worst was over now, and I had not in any case much farther to go. When I got to the site, I put the timber down beside its fellow. I never even switched off the torch. I took it off my neck and held it in my hand. Then I went straight back into the wood.

I do not know how long the whole thing took. It seemed a very long time, but I think in fact I made very good speed. When I came to the clearing for the third time, I was too much taken up with my physical distress for the beastliness of the place to touch me. I carried the timber to the edge of the ditch and let it fall anyhow across the others. There was no more nicety left in me. I went down to the tent. I did not want to eat anything. I drank some water and got into my bag, but now I could not sleep. I do not think I slept again properly until the whole action was played out. The wind roared in the wood all night. If anything moved over the leaves on top of the bank, I did not hear it. As soon as it was light enough, I got up and made myself some tea. I found I could eat after that. My heart was not much in it, but I ate what I could. Then I went up and began putting the gyn together. I was at it most of the day.

The last night I hardly remember at all. I know the wind had gone down and the wood was quiet again. I must have made three journeys to the shed, because what I had to bring could not have taken less, but the loads were lighter. In any case, I was never really conscious of feeling physically tired. Somewhere in the dead hours before the morning I put the maul and the hooked spikes down behind the winch. Further along the rest of the tackle lay ready to be rigged, and beyond it the gaunt tripod of the gyn stood up over the stone. The labor was over. From now on I only had to be clever. But I had to be clever quickly, because tomorrow was the fourth day.

This time I was wide awake when I heard the noise of the leaves. The wood was quiet, too. The noise came very faintly at first. I could not have heard it at all if the silence had not been so complete. It grew louder almost at once, as if whatever was making it was getting nearer. It was a steady threshing of the drifted leaves, that passed along the bank above the tent and died away again in the silence. I lay on my back with my eyes open, staring up at the barely visible line of the tent ridge. I did not know what made the sound, but it did not worry me. My mind was busy on block and tackle, almost my eyes as well in the intense visual imagination of overtiredness. I went through the whole process in my mind several times, checking and improving, up to the point when I could start winching the stone up out of its pit. Beyond that my mind would not go. I must have shut my eyes and dozed off at some point, because I was never conscious of its getting light. I merely noticed suddenly that it was, but it did not feel like waking up.

CHAPTER 18

WHEN THE DAY CAME UP, it was another of those golden autumn days of pale sunshine and motionless air. It was the last we had that year. Even the oaks had lost most of their leaves now, and the sunlight filtered down into the wood, so that on the top of the bank I could feel it at times warm on my skin. I wondered whether Cynthia would go walking on the hills, and if she did, whether she would climb up to our shelf on the hillside. I remembered, as a fact, lying beside her there on another such golden day as this, but I could not connect the memory very directly with my present experience. It was like something you remember doing years ago, perhaps in your childhood. You know that the person who did it must have been you, but you cannot make any solid identification of him with your present self. The thing I remembered was only a week or so ago, but already it felt like that. In any case, I did not remember it very vividly or for very long. It just came into my mind for a moment while I was wrestling with the wire rope. I suppose it was the smell of the autumn wood and the sunlight on my face.

Wire ropes, even when they are new as this one was, are nasty things to handle, but that was one of the things I had thought of before I left the flat. I had brought a pair of solid leather gloves with me. I knew already how I was going to rig the tackle between the winch and the gyn. It was getting an adequate sling round the stone that I had to experiment with, and I spent a long time over it. To start with I had to dig under the far end of the stone until I could get a length of rope under it with plenty to spare on both sides of the pit. I did not like working under the stone at all, even to this extent, but I had to do it. Once I had got the rope well under, I could pull it first from one side and then from the other, and always along toward the center of the stone, so that it gradually sawed its way through the soil underneath. I knew how far I had to get it because of the marks on the sides of the stone. In this as in much else I was content merely to reproduce the operation that had already been done once. Dick was not an engineer, but he had picked my brains often enough on things of this sort. Also, knowing what I now knew, I did not doubt that this was an operation he was already familiar with, and might even have had practical experience of. I felt sure he had got the stone up clear of the bottom of the pit, but I did not know what had happened after that.

What I was not really sure of was what would happen when the stone was partially up. I had got the gyn placed so as to exert the most effective pull to start the stone swinging up on its pointed end, but its angle would change as it came up, and I could not change the position of the gyn. The rope would not have much hold on the damp rounded surfaces. I was afraid that at some point the sling might tend to slip upward suddenly, and I did not know what would happen if it did. I thought this was where the prop would come in, only I doubted if even the prop could hold the stone against a sudden lurch. But there was nothing for it but to try.

By midday the whole thing was rigged. I took up enough rope to lift the tackle clear of the ground between the winch and the gyn, but not enough to put any real strain on it. A few more turns would do it. I was ready to begin lifting the stone. This was the point I had reached in my imagination, but I had never got beyond it. I left everything as it was and went down to the tent. I told myself it was time I had something to eat, but I had not the smallest wish to eat. It was just that, now that I had come up to it, I could not face what I had to do.

It was my old obsession with time that got me moving again. I thought that something might go wrong, the stone might slip or the tackle give at some point. Then I should have to start all over again, and the day was half gone already. I gave up pretending I wanted to eat. I went back and began winding in what was left of the slack. The rope came taut, and the gyn creaked, shifted slightly and settled down to take the strain. I went on winding. It was not hard work after what I had been doing the last four days.

I kept my eyes on the earth beyond the gyn. I could not see the stone from here. All I could see was the lip of the pit, with the heaped earth beyond it and on both sides of it. The ropes were as taut as steel rods now. The reduction was so great that you could not see the blocks turning. The whole thing looked static and rigid. There did not seem to be any movement anywhere, but there must be movement. Inch by inch the rope was coming on to the drum, and it must be coming from somewhere. There was a faint final complaint from the top of the gyn, but there was nothing to see there. When I looked down again, there it was. There was a grayish curve showing just above the surface. You could see it against the brown of the heaped earth. It glistened slightly in the sunlight, as if its ancient surfaces were sticky with the damp and slime of the pit. The stone was starting to lift.

I went on winding until the far end of the stone

looked a foot or so above the surface. As it had started a foot or more below it, the bottom of the stone must have lifted a couple of feet from the bottom of the pit, but only at the far end. At the near end it would have sunk if anything as the pointed end of the stone began to turn down into what may have been its original socket. I left the winch and went along to the stone. I walked down the side of the ditch and along under it and then up again. I was not going to walk close to the wire ropes, even at this degree of tension. If they do part, they can do horrible damage.

The stone was coming up just as I had thought it would and as it probably had before. Its huge blind head was cocked up out of the earth like some sort of monstrous reptile that had been too long underground. The walls of the pit stood up close round it. There was only darkness under it and the smell of damp soil. It had a long way to come yet before I could see clear to the bottom of the pit. I went back to the winch, down the slope, along the ditch, up the slope again. Then I went on winding.

Even from where I was the stone looked horrible as it came up. If it had stood out all these years in the weather, as it should have done, it would have looked rugged and clean, but now it was blotchy and foul with the puddled earth of the bank. Also, it looked bigger, much bigger than it had lying flat in its burial pit. It rose very, very slowly. It was a monstrous, menacing object. I was just going to go along for another look at it when the wire sling slipped for the first time.

It was only a slight slip, just the sling settling to a new angle, but it was frightening all the same. The whole contraption thudded as the shock passed through it. I had stopped winding before it happened, but now I went on again for a little, to take up the rope the stone had let slip and get the sling tightened hard on its new position. When I thought the stone had made up the lost height, I stopped winding and went along to the pit.

At the far end, the bottom of the stone was now just clear of the edge of the pit. I could see about half the bottom of the pit, but only obliquely and only by crouching and peering in under the huge hanging head of the stone. From there there was nothing to see but earth. The earth was rammed down and molded by the weight of the stone, but I did not think it was the original bottom of the pit, not quite. It looked as if a certain amount of fresh earth had fallen in from the sides of the pit when the stone had been raised the first time. I could not tell how much there was of it. All I knew was that what I could see was not the surface the stone had lain on all those centuries since the monks had toppled it over. And I could not see more than half of it, even so. The stone had to come up a lot more yet. I went back to the winch, avoiding the ropes now more than ever, and started winding again.

The stone must have been up to nearly sixty degrees before the sling slipped the second time. Once more I wound up a little and then went along to see the position. I did not like what I saw. The gyn was pulling the sling too much upward, and at the angle the stone was now lying it would not take much to pull it up over the head of the stone altogether. I thought that if nothing disturbed it, it would hold at its present angle, but I did not think it would be safe to try to take it any higher. I went back for the prop and took it to the far end of the pit. I dropped one end into the pit and butted it firmly against the bottom of the end wall. Then I let the other end swing in until it jammed under the overhanging bottom of the stone. I got the whole thing as central as I could, and drove it in tight under the stone with my heel, while I balanced precariously on the undisturbed soil at the end of the pit. I thought merely that it would take some of the weight of the stone and make the sling less likely to slip off altogether. In fact I must have done a better job than I imagined.

But this, finally and unarguably, was as far as I could go with the thing. This was the end of my four days' sweat and contriving. The stone was up as far as it would go. There was nothing left now but to see what I had done all this to see, if it was there to be seen. I left the end of the pit and went round to the eastern side of it. Then I got down on my hands and knees and crawled to the edge. I could see pretty well the whole bottom of the pit now. It was molded in folds and ridges to the shape of the weathered stone. Everything was earth-colored, but it was not all earth. There were other things showing among the earth. They might be stones or bits of wood or even tree roots. They might be anything that was not earth. I could not be certain what they were. I leant forward as far as I could, peering into the pit, with the huge mottled stone hanging over me. The edge of the pit was not altogether firm, and once the soil gave way under my hand as I craned forward, so that for a moment I thought I was going to pitch head-first into the bottom. I recovered myself and sat back on my heels. My mouth was dry, but the sweat ran down my back under my shirt. I knew what I had to do, and I could not bear the thought of it. I had to go down into the pit and see what there was down there among the rammed earth that was not earth.

I looked at the ropes strained taut and motionless between the winch and the gyn. I looked at the gyn itself, with its straddled feet driven down into the top of the bank by the downward drag of the forces balanced over its central block. I looked longest at the sling of wire rope caught round the hanging head of the stone. It would not take much to have it off, but it would take something. Left undisturbed, the whole monstrous box of tricks would stay in balance. And there was nothing to disturb it. Nothing moved in the wood, no wind stirred in the trees. The stone might hang over its pit for days. There was no reason why it should come down just because I was underneath it. In any case, there was nothing else I could do. I took my knife out of my pocket and opened the long blade. Then, with the open knife in my hand, I got down on my hands and knees and slithered over the edge of the pit.

Everything was sticky and slippery under me, and the air was full of the damp sour smell of the midden or the bog. The earth walls stood up all round and the immense sweating roof of stone hung overhead. I could see sky only at the far end of the pit, where the stone was highest. I forced myself to look down at what was underneath me. I began prodding and ferreting among the slimy earth with the blade of my knife. I do not know how long this went on. It cannot have been very long, because there was not really a very big area to cover. Then the soil fell away from something brown and solid, and I saw it was the heel of a shoe. I scraped away a little more earth with the knife and took hold of it. I tried to pull it out of the earth, but it would not move at all. It was anchored down into the earth by what was inside it. Then the stone moved and I heard the wire sling whip off the top of it.

The stone lurched sideways and downward a little and came to rest on the prop. The prop held. I did not think at all. I began to crawl toward the far end of the pit. I think I made instinctively for the daylight. The side would have been nearer. In fact what I did offered the least chance of disturbing the stone. I got to the end and put my hands up on to the dry earth at the edge of the pit. Then I raised myself on my knees, keeping my head down as much as I could, and slithered out into the daylight.

I lay for a moment face down on the earth. Then I turned over and sat up. All I could see was the stone, slightly askew now, but still hanging over the pit with only the prop holding it. When I got to my feet, I could see over the stone. Merrion was standing between me and the winch. He was looking down at the coils of wire rope and tackle lying along the top of the bank at his feet. He lifted a hand to his mouth and I saw it was bleeding steadily. Then he turned and saw me looking at him.

He must have known it would be me. He must have known I should crawl out of the pit some time, because the stone had not fallen. All the same, he looked at me as if he did not fully believe what he saw. He could not have been there very long, of course. I can see now, looking at the thing from this distance of time, that the mere finding of the stone lifted out of its pit again must have been almost enough to upset his reason. Unless I was mistaken, his reason was pretty precariously balanced already. For a moment or two we looked at each other across the top of the hanging stone. Then he turned and came very slowly toward me. His hands hung loose at his sides. He had nothing in them, but one of them still dripped blood. I think I looked round for a weapon of some sort, but there was nothing. I had dropped the knife, such as it was, in the bottom of the pit.

He did not say anything. He was very good at not saying anything, and in any case there was not really anything either of us could say. I still did not know what he was going to do. I had moved round to the side of the pit by now. There was nothing between us but the trampled edge of the ditch and the line of heaped earth I had taken out of the side of the pit. Halfway along the line there was the gap I had left so that I could get the gear to the pit. Merrion came on quite slowly, with his head lowered, looking up at me with his staring gray eyes under his dark brows. He looked for all the world like an animal making up its mind to charge. Having nothing but my hands, I clenched them instinctively into fists, tucking the thumbs well under, so that I could hit without hurting them. I noticed, too late, that his hands were hanging loose and open. When he did come at me, he stooped at the last moment, ducked under my guard and caught me round the waist.

He was much stronger than he looked and much heavier than I was. I think he must have been a rugby forward in his youth. He knew exactly what he wanted to do and how to do it. He ran me backward steadily toward the side of the pit, his feet in their town shoes digging savagely into the soft earth behind him. I hit him repeatedly on the head. His head was tucked down by my waist, and I remember noticing with a curious distaste that there was a round bald patch on the crown. You never see a thing like that with a man as tall as he was. He felt soft and heavy and enormously powerful. I detested the whole feel of him. Even apart from sheer fright, I wanted desperately to get away from him. I checked his rush just before we got to the gap in the piled earth, and for a moment we hung there, grunting like animals.

I knew there was only one way to make him loosen his hold. Hitting the top of a man's head with your fist only hurts your fist. I had to go for his eyes. I loathed the thought of it, but there was nothing else to do. I put my hand down and felt with my fingers under his downturned face, groping for the eye-sockets. He butted savagely forward again, but I jinked sideways, and his thrust carried us along the side of the pit instead of back toward it. My groping fingers found his eye, and he turned his face against my side to avoid them. It was that that finished him, because he could not see where we were or what he was doing.

His threshing left foot got on to the brittle soil on the lip of the pit, and a moment later the soil gave way under it. The foot went over the edge, and his whole body sagged suddenly, so that instead of pushing me backward, he was dragging me forward toward him. I swung him, trying to tear myself away from him, and his other foot went over. He came down on his knees, with his back almost under the hanging edge of the stone. He let go of me then. He had to. He put his hands down, scrabbling at the soft soil to save himself, but he was too far off balance. I jerked myself clear of him, stumbled on the heaped soil and came down on all fours, still facing him.

For a moment we crouched there, staring at each other, both on our knees, more like animals than ever. Then his hands lost their grip and his weight carried him backward. He somersaulted clean over, and I heard something, I think it must have been his head, hit the prop. It hit it with a clear smack, and the prop went over sideways.

The stone did not fall. That was the appalling thing. It settled. It came down, almost slowly, but quite inexorably, pivoting on its sharp end. I heard him scream once, as the barber-surgeon must have screamed, and then the scream was cut off short by the tremendous thud of the stone. When I got to my feet, the stone was back in its pit. I could just see the end of the prop sticking up out of the far side of the pit, but there was nothing else to see at all, only the stone and the trampled earth all round it.

CHAPTER 19

I TURNED AND WALKED to the edge of the ditch. Then I dropped on my knees again and tried very hard to vomit. I did not succeed very well because my stomach had nothing in it to throw up. After a bit the retching stopped. I wiped away the slime which was about all I had been able to get rid of and threw the screwed-up handkerchief into the trampled earth behind me. Then I went straight on into the wood. I knew the way by now, but I saw my blazes on the trees on each side of me. I supposed that Merrion must have seen them too when he came this way. He would have known then that something was up, even before he saw the bank. That would have been the first thing he really did know. I did not imagine he would have looked in the shed before he came along.

I walked through the clearing where the church had been without really looking at it. It was full of the pale yellow sunlight and completely still. Even at this time of the year there should have been some birds singing somewhere, but there were none. I passed the dancing man's stone without looking at it either. I had my eyes on the ground. I cannot really say what I was thinking. I know there was an element of enormous immediate relief in my mind, but beyond it an enormous apprehension. When I raised my eyes, I saw Ethel Merrion coming to meet me along the track. She was already quite close. I stopped and let her come to me. She moved quickly, as always. She came up to me and said, "Is he dead?" It was only later I discovered that the lower half of me was covered with blood from Merrion's damaged hand, but at the time the question did not strike me as odd.

I nodded. "Under the stone," I said. "That was an accident, but he had attacked me. Dick's there too. I don't know whether that was an accident or not."

She frowned and her eyes went away past me. She was looking at the standing stone by the track behind me. She said, "Under the stone?"

"Not that one," I said. "There's another. It was buried by the ditch. They'd dug it up." I knew this was no good as an explanation, but I could not make the effort to do any better.

She did not really want to know, in any case. She had already asked the only question she wanted answered. She brought her eyes back to me again. "What are you going to do?" she said.

"I don't know. Tell the police, I suppose. It's up to you, really. It's your place now."

She shook her head. She was as quick and incisive as ever. "Not mine, no. It's Cynthia's. I've got the Bristol house. That was agreed. It's her home, after all."

"Cynthia's? Llanglas is Cynthia's?" She nodded. "Where is she?" I said. "At the house?"

"Not when we got here. I don't know where she is. Out, somewhere. The house is open."

"I'd better go," I said. I thought for a moment. I said, "Why did you come back now?"

"I don't know. We came in a hurry. I think Roger had a letter."

I could not understand that. I shook my head but did not say anything. It was only later I thought of old

Evans. She reached a hand up and touched me gently on the arm. "You go," she said. "You're not hurt?"

"I'm not hurt, no. Will you be all right?"

She looked puzzled at this, almost impatient. She said, "Of course I'll be all right." She left me and walked on. I think she was going to the dancing man's stone. I went on toward the house.

There was no one about when I got there. Merrion's car was standing on the gravel in front. The driving door was wide open, as if he had jumped out of it as soon as the car had stopped. The nearside door was shut. I went across the gravel and into the house. It was completely quiet here too. I looked into the kitchen, but there was no one there. I went upstairs and along the corridor to Cynthia's room. The door was shut. I knew she was not there. I opened the door and put my head inside. It still smelt faintly of her. It was all very orderly. It was difficult to believe that my clothes and hers had once been scattered all over the floor. I shut the door and went back along the corridor. Just before I got to the top of the stairs, I heard her in the hall below. She called, "Roger! Roger! Where are you?"

I came out on the top of the stairs, and she was at the bottom, looking up at me.

She said, "You! What— Did you come with Roger?"

"No," I said, "I didn't come with him." I started to go downstairs, and she must have seen the state I was in.

She said, "What's the matter? What's happened? Are you all right?"

When I got to the bottom, she reached out and took my hands. I did not like letting her take them, but I let her. She knew something was wrong, of course. For a moment I held her hands and looked at her. There was a sort of glow about her. I think she had been out walking on the hills while I had been digging a pit for her brother in the wood. My one conscious emotion was an almost unbearable fear of losing her. I said, "I've got to tell you. Where can we go? In the kitchen?"

"All right." She let go of my hands and turned and went across the hall. I went after her. "Where's Roger?" she said.

I shut the door of the kitchen behind us. She stood by the table looking at me. I think she knew what I was going to say. "Roger's dead," I said.

She did not take her eyes off mine. I have never been subjected to such a fearful scrutiny. She said, "Did you kill him?"

"No. No, I didn't kill him. He—he killed himself, in a way. He didn't mean to, of course."

For a moment she did not say anything. She just went on looking at me. When she did speak, it was hardly above a whisper. "Oh, thank God," she said.

Only then she took her eyes off mine. She turned and pulled out a chair and sat down at the table. "Sit down," she said. "Tell me what happened." She was completely in control again, of me and of herself. I pulled out another chair and sat facing her. There was something curiously formal about the whole thing, but I was glad of it.

I said, "There are things we must tell each other."

She nodded. "You are all right?" she said. "You're not hurt?" It was only then, when I sat down, that I saw the blood on my clothes.

"I'm all right," I said.

She nodded. "Tell me, then," she said. I was wondering where to begin when she said suddenly, "Where's Ethel?"

"She's in the wood."

She said, "Is she with Roger?"

"No. No, she's alone."

She nodded. "Go on," she said.

I told her the whole thing, or my side of it, right

through from the beginning. She did not interrupt at all. She did not look at me while I was speaking. Mostly she looked at her hands, which were clasped in front of her on the table. When I had finished she drew a very long breath. She still sat there, looking at her hands. I simply waited. You used to read in books about a man finding his whole life hanging on what another person was going to say. I had never imagined what it would feel like in practice. I knew that, whatever she said, there would be no taking it back.

She did not say it, not all at once. She said, "I've always—looked after him, you see? He needed looking after."

"I know that," I said. "You didn't know what had happened to Dick?"

"I knew he hadn't been lost climbing. Roger said he'd never be found, but that's all he'd tell me. It was desperately important to him that the truth shouldn't come out. He said it had been an accident, of course. I believed him. I had to. You don't?"

"I don't know. I know he tried to kill me today in the same way as Dick had been killed. But of course by then he'd put himself in the wrong by concealing Dick's death. Or falsifying it, anyhow. But I can imagine his wanting Dick out of the way. Still, we'll never know. Not now. He got Dick here, didn't he?"

"Yes. He'd found this thing, you see, but it was outside his own field. He didn't tell me much. He never told anyone more than he could help about anything. He just said there was this prehistoric thing there that might be important. He'd already met your brother. He got him in—I think he thought he'd be an easy man to handle. Then later, when they found out how enormously important it was—he found he wasn't. Not in any way."

"He underestimated him," I said. "We all did. That was half the trouble. He put on this playboy act. Well—

he was a playboy in some ways. But not over his work. All the same, your brother's attitude wasn't—well, normal, you know."

"I know that. But when the thing was done, what could I do? I didn't like your brother. He had threatened Roger's happiness in more than one way. It's no good, Mark. I thought we were well rid of him. So I did what Roger wanted. The one thing that might have made me decide differently I didn't know about. I couldn't."

"What was that?" I said.

She got up and went over to the window. She stood there for a moment, looking out. The sunlight had gone now. All the hillsides were gray with the beginning of evening. Then she turned and faced me. "You," she said.

I knew then. I knew by the way she said that one word. "Go on," I said.

"When you came, and I found you were the person you are, I saw what I'd done. Then later I thought—I suppose I thought I could have it both ways. I thought I could keep Roger's secret and keep you, too. I wanted to, more than I had ever wanted anything. I suppose I underestimated you, too. I'm sorry."

I said, "I had to know. You can see that? Apart from anything else, I had to know because of you. I couldn't let the thing lie between us as it was. I knew what I was risking. I knew I might lose you in the process. But I still had to go on with it."

She had turned and was looking out of the window again. I got up and went to her. She said, "Don't touch me, please. Promise you won't touch me."

"I won't touch you," I said. "But you must make up your mind."

"About what?" She turned and looked at me. She really did not understand.

"About me. Whether you want me after all this."

Quite suddenly she smiled. She said, "Dear Mark, of course I want you. I shall never want anything else. Whether you want me or not, I shall go on wanting you."

"And I you," I said.

She said, "That's all right, then. Now what are you going to do?"

"I'm going out to get myself some clean clothes. Then we're going to phone the police."

She nodded. "Go on, then," she said. I turned and left her standing there by the window. I went straight out of the house and back along the track into the wood. The air was chilly now, and there was mist rising under the trees. I knew I was cold, but nothing mattered at all. It never occurred to me that I might meet Ethel Merrion, and I did not. I do not know where she was, but she was not by the standing stone. The dancing man would still be capering on its western face, but I did not go over to see. I saw the flowers as I went by, but I left them where they were. There was no one in the wood at all now. There were two men under the stone, Cynthia's brother and mine, but they were both dead. The monks were there, or some of them, but they were dead, too, long dead. I supposed before very long there would be people in the wood, policemen with notebooks and photographers with cameras, but there would not be very much they could do tonight and I did not think they would stay very long. Then just before morning there would be others, that only I knew about. They would come walking over the dead leaves, beating the bounds of their mystery, because whatever it was they had put here was too important to let them forget it altogether, even in four thousand years. But tonight there would be no one to hear them go by.